AA

Please return this book on or before the date shown above. To
renew go to www.essex.gov.uk/libraries, ring 0845 603 7628 or
go to any Essex library.

M

Essex County Council

D0261326

'Hayley—' Trying to think cold thoughts to relieve the throbbing ache in his body, Patrick focused on the conversation and not her mouth. **'It's Christmas Eve. You came all this way to find me—'**

'Could you stop rubbing it in?'

'—and now you're planning to leave.'

'Yes.'

'Have you given any thought to where you're going to go?'

'No. Somewhere…' She gave a defensive shrug. 'Somewhere nice. With a big Christmas tree. And very possibly a log fire.'

'We have a big tree here. And a log fire.'

'Somewhere with a big tree and a log fire *where you don't live.*'

'Hayley, it's Christmas Eve,' he said again gently.

She'd come all this way to see him again—his hand closed around her wrist and he felt the instant charge of electricity that had connected them from the first moment—*and he wasn't going to let her leave.*

'If I ask you something, will you answer me honestly?' He slid his hand behind her head, his eyes locked with hers.

'What?'

He gave a slow smile. 'Can you really cook a turkey?'

MISTLETOE & MATERNITY

Marriages made under the mistletoe

Snowflakes are starting to fall, Christmas carols are ringing out, and for the Buchannan brothers there are festive surprises in store…

These two gorgeous and dedicated doctors lost their faith in love a long time ago, but they're about to meet the women who can unlock their hearts and give them the most precious gift of all…

A family—just in time for Christmas!

Bestselling author Sarah Morgan brings you a brand-new duet full of all the magic of Christmas!

SNOWBOUND: MIRACLE MARRIAGE

and

CHRISTMAS EVE: DOORSTEP DELIVERY

Both available this month from Mills & Boon® Medical™ Romance

CHRISTMAS EVE: DOORSTEP DELIVERY

BY
SARAH MORGAN

MILLS & BOON

All the characters in this book have no existence outside
the imagination of the author, and have no relation
whatsoever to anyone bearing the same name or names.
They are not even distantly inspired by any individual
known or unknown to the author, and all the incidents
are pure invention.

First published in Great Britain 2009
Large Print edition 2010
Harlequin Mills & Boon Limited,
Eton House, 18-24 Paradise Road,
Richmond, Surrey TW9 1SR

© Sarah Morgan 2009

ISBN: 978 0 263 21090 3

Harlequin Mills & Boon policy is to use papers that are
natural, renewable and recyclable products and made
from wood grown in sustainable forests. The logging and
manufacturing process conform to the legal environmental
regulations of the country of origin.

Printed and bound in Great Britain
by CPI Antony Rowe, Chippenham, Wiltshire

Sarah Morgan is a British writer who regularly tops the bestseller lists with her lively stories for both Mills & Boon® Medical™ and Modern™.

As a child Sarah dreamed of being a writer, and although she took a few interesting detours on the way she is now living that dream. She firmly believes that reading romance is one of the most satisfying and fat-free escapist pleasures available. Her stories are unashamedly optimistic, and she is always pleased when she receives letters from readers saying that her books have helped them through hard times.

RT Book Reviews has described her writing as 'action-packed and sexy'.

Sarah lives near London with her husband and two children, who innocently provide an endless supply of authentic dialogue. When she isn't writing or nagging about homework Sarah enjoys music, movies, and any activity that takes her outdoors.

Recent titles by the same author:

Medical™ Romance
THE GREEK BILLIONAIRE'S LOVE-CHILD
ITALIAN DOCTOR, SLEIGH-BELL BRIDE
THE REBEL DOCTOR'S BRIDE**
THE ITALIAN'S NEW-YEAR MARRIAGE WISH*

Brides of Penhally Bay
**Glenmore Island Doctors*

Sarah Morgan also writes for Modern™ Romance. Her sexy heroes and feisty heroines aren't to be missed!

Modern™ Romance
POWERFUL GREEK, UNWORLDLY WIFE
CAPELLI'S CAPTIVE VIRGIN
THE PRINCE'S WAITRESS WIFE

PROLOGUE

PATRICK strode through the doors of the labour ward, his bleep and his phone buzzing simultaneously. Pushing open the doors of the delivery room, he walked straight into an atmosphere of palpable tension.

His eyes met those of a white-faced midwife. Despite the soothing words she was muttering to the panicking mother, there was no missing the strain in her expression and her relief at seeing him.

'Cord prolapse, Patrick. The trace has shown persistent variable decelerations and prolonged bradychardia. I've put her in the knee-elbow position, they're preparing Theatre and I've emergency-bleeped the anaesthetist. I'm so sorry to drag you out of your meeting. I know the chief exec gets furious when you go running off.'

'It's not a problem.' Patrick shrugged off the jacket of his suit, slung it over the back of the nearest chair and unbuttoned his shirtsleeves. 'Ed?' He turned to his registrar and noticed that he looked unusually stressed.

'She needs a crash section,' his colleague muttered in an undertone. 'After I called you, I put a line in and infused 50 mils of saline into her bladder, as you instructed. Did I miss anything?'

'Did you do an ultrasound?'

'Yes. There's good blood flow through the cord.'

'All right. Good job. So we've bought ourselves some time.' Patrick rolled up the sleeves of his shirt. 'You say she isn't suitable for a general anaesthetic?'

'That's right.' The registrar handed him the notes but Patrick gave a brief shake of his head and walked to the head of the bed.

'Hello, Katherine. I'm Patrick Buchannan, one of the obstetric consultants.'

'I know what you're going to say and I don't want a Caesarean section,' the mother wailed. 'I want to have this baby naturally. That's why I only came into hospital half an hour ago. I knew this would happen. I knew if I came in earlier, you'd muck about with me.' She was kneeling face down on the trolley, her bottom in the air in an attempt to prevent the cord being compressed between the pelvis and the baby's head. 'I feel ridiculous in this position. It's so undignified.'

'This position is saving your baby's life.' Patrick squatted down next to her so that he could have a proper conversation and build a connection with the labouring woman. 'Do you understand what is happening, Katherine?'

'Yes. You're going to cut me open instead of letting me have the baby the way nature intended!' The woman was sobbing now, her head on her arms. 'I hate you. I hate you all. Oh God, why did this have to happen?'

'You're very tired, Katherine.' Patrick spoke gently. 'From what I've been told, you were in labour for a long time at home before you came to us.'

'I didn't want to come to you at all! I just want to have the baby naturally.'

Seeing how terrified she was, Patrick felt his heart twist in sympathy. 'You can't have this baby naturally, sweetheart. It's too much of a risk. The cord is prolapsed—that means that it's dropped down below the baby's head. That's why you're lying in this undignified position. The cord is your baby's blood supply—if that blood supply is obstructed, the baby could die.'

Katherine gave a low moan and turned her blotched, tear-streaked face to him. 'Don't say that! *Don't say that!*'

'It's the truth. And I won't lie to you.'

'You're putting pressure on me to have the one thing I don't want!'

'I'm putting pressure on you, that's true—but because this is a medical emergency, not for any other reason.'

'You're a surgeon. You'd much rather intervene than let women do it by themselves.'

'I'm the last person in the world to intervene surgically when there is another option.' Patrick spoke quietly, holding up his hand to silence his registrar, who had drawn breath to speak. 'Katherine, if I thought you could deliver this baby yourself, I'd let you do it.'

Katherine sniffed, but she kept her eyes on his, desperate for reassurance and guarantees. 'How do I know you don't just want to get home in time for Christmas?'

Patrick smiled. 'Because it isn't Christmas Eve until tomorrow. I've done all my shopping, the turkey is in the fridge and my kids don't want me home until they've 'secretly' wrapped my presents. If I turn up now, I'll be in trouble.'

Katherine's breath was jerky from crying. 'I can't have a general anaesthetic.'

'So I understand. Don't worry. I know the whole thing sounds scary and you feel out of control.' Patrick rubbed his hand over her shoulder to reassure her. 'I'm going to ask you to trust me to do what's best for you. Can you do that? I promise you that everything I do will be for you and the baby. Not for me.'

'If I can't have an anaesthetic—'

'We'll give you a spinal. You won't feel any pain, I promise.'

'Is that like an epidural?'

'Similar.' Keeping his hand on her shoulder Patrick stood up, his gaze flickering to the senior midwife in the room. 'Is the anaesthetist on his way?'

'He's meeting us in Theatre,' the registrar said, and then lowered his voice. 'Can he put in a spinal when she's in the Trendelenberg position?'

'Who is the anaesthetist?'

'Gary Clarke.'

Patrick gave a faint smile. 'Gary could put in a spinal if she was hanging from the ceiling. I'm going to go and scrub. I'll see you in there.'

Katherine gave a little moan. 'It's going to go wrong. I know it is.'

'No, it isn't.' Maggie, the senior midwife, took over the role of offering moral support. 'Patrick is the best there is. He'll have your baby safely delivered in less time than it takes you to make a cup of tea. Come on, now, love. I know it isn't what you planned, but you have to think of the baby.'

'Kathy.' Her husband added his pleas, 'I know you're scared but you have to do this.'

Katherine looked at Maggie, panic in her eyes. 'Would you let him deliver your baby?'

'Patrick *did* deliver my baby,' Maggie said gruffly. 'I had a condition called placenta praevia, which is when the placenta is lying across the cervix. Patrick did my Caesarean section. And that was seven years ago when he was still a registrar. He was brilliant even then, and he's had tons of practice since.'

Katherine gave a choked laugh. 'Perhaps you should start a fan club for him.'

'I'm too late. If you go on the internet you'll find loads of threads devoted to chatting about how brilliant he is. We get women coming up from London just to see him because he's an expert in premature labour. You see? He can even teach those London doctors a thing or two.'

Katherine groaned. 'It's just that I hate needles, I hate operations.' She hiccoughed. 'I hate—'

Knowing that he couldn't proceed until the anaesthetist arrived, Patrick turned his attention back to the labouring woman. 'It's difficult when things don't go the way you planned. I understand that. When my daughter was born the whole thing was a nightmare from beginning to end, and I'm an obstetrician. Nothing went the way I wanted it to go.'

He didn't add that his wife had blamed him.

Ex-wife, he reminded himself wearily. She was his ex-wife.

Katherine's face was discoloured from crying, her eyes tired after a long labour. 'I wanted to have this baby at home.'

'And having a baby at home can be a wonderful experience, but there are certain times when that just isn't safe,' Patrick said softly, 'and this is one of them.'

She gave a strangled laugh. 'I thought you'd lecture me for staying at home for so long.'

It wasn't the time to tell her she should have come into hospital hours ago. What was the point in adding to her guilt and worry? What he really needed to do was gain her confidence. 'I'm a great supporter of home birth, providing the circumstances are right. This isn't one of those circumstances.'

Katherine looked at him, exhausted, confused and wrung out by the whole physical and emotional experience of childbirth. 'I don't want anything to happen to the baby.'

'I know you don't.' Patrick watched as the foetal heart monitor showed another dip. 'The baby isn't happy, Katherine. We need to do this, and we need to do it now. Maggie, can you bleep Gary again? Tell him I want him up here any time in the next two seconds. The rest of you—transfer her into Theatre while I go and scrub. Move.'

Patrick changed quickly and then started to

scrub, allowing the hot soapy water to drain down his arms.

'She's ready.' Another the midwife hurried up to him. 'We've taken blood for cross-matching and she's breathing 100 per cent oxygen. Gary is doing a spinal. He says can you please start soon because he's getting bored.'

Patrick gave a smile of appreciation and moments later he was gloved and gowned, scalpel in hand. 'If you need any advice, Gary, just let me know,' he said smoothly, exchanging a glance with his colleague. 'Katherine, if you feel anything at any point, you just tell me. Are you all ready for Christmas?' He chatted easily, the words requiring no concentration, all his focus on the technical operation he was performing. Even though the foetal heart was stable, he knew that time wasn't on his side.

He also knew that he didn't intend to lose this baby.

'I've bought the presents.' Katherine's voice was wobbly with nerves. 'I'm supposed to be picking up the turkey tomorrow.'

The staff draped sterile cloths in such a way that Katherine couldn't see what was happening.

'Someone else can do that for you—it will be good practice for your husband.' Patrick held out his gloved hand and the midwife assisting him passed him the instrument he needed. 'Any tips on cooking turkey are gratefully received. Last year it was a disaster, I ended up cooking cranberry omelette. My children have never forgiven me.' His gloved fingers widened the incision he'd made and he glanced at the clock. Three minutes.

The door to Theatre opened and the paediatrician hurried into the room, ready to take the baby.

'Good timing. Come on, little fellow.' Patrick eased the baby out and there was a collective sigh of relief when the child started to bawl loudly. 'You have a son, Katherine. Merry Christmas.' He allowed the mother to see and touch the baby briefly before handing the boy to the hovering paediatrician. 'Nothing to worry about. We just need to check him over, Katherine.'

Leaving the baby in the hands of his colleague, Patrick turned his attention back to his own job. Delivering the placenta and then closing. He worked quickly and quietly, aware of Katherine and her husband in the background talking in low, excited voices.

'That was fast, even for you.' Watching him close, Maggie opened another suture for him. 'A new record. I think you could just be a genius.'

Patrick grinned. 'I do love a bit of hero-worship. Does all this admiration mean you're willing to perform that traditional midwifery task of making me a cup of tea when I've finished here?'

'Don't push your luck, handsome. I didn't train for all those years to make you tea.' Maggie handed him a swab. 'And, anyway, you won't have time to drink it.'

'That's probably true.'

'I don't know why you're complaining. You have Christmas off.'

Patrick's fingers worked swiftly and skilfully. 'This will be my first Christmas at home with my kids in years.'

'Want me to come and cook that turkey for you?' Maggie winked saucily and Patrick smiled.

'You're happily married. Behave yourself.'

Watching what he was doing, she opened a sterile dressing. 'Tom Hunter is on call over Christmas. If his wife delivers, you might have to come in anyway. He doesn't trust anyone else.

He's going to have a nervous breakdown if you're not here.'

'I saw Sally in clinic today. She won't deliver until Boxing Day at the earliest.' Patrick secured the dressing. 'This year, I'm going to eat my turkey in peace. That's if I manage to work out how to cook the damn thing. Katherine. I'm done here.' He smiled at the patient. 'I'm going to get cleaned up, we'll transfer you to the ward and then I'll come and see you.'

The woman's eyes were misted with tears of gratitude and euphoria. 'Thank you. Thank you for saving my baby—and thank you for making the whole thing so unscary. I'm sorry I was so pathetic. You are a fantastic doctor and your wife is a lucky woman.'

There was sudden tension in the operating theatre and several of the staff exchanged embarrassed glances, but Patrick simply smiled.

'Unfortunately my now ex-wife would have disagreed with you,' he drawled, stepping back from the operating table and ripping off his gloves. 'She would have been the first to tell you that fantastic doctors make lousy husbands. I'll see you later, Katherine. I'll be in my office if anyone needs me.'

He stayed longer in the shower than he should have done, feeling the hot water sluice over his bare flesh while he tried shut down his thinking.

Lousy husband.

That was what he'd been to Carly, wasn't it?

Feeling the familiar stab of guilt, he turned off the water and cursed softly.

He'd already promised himself that he wasn't going to spend another Christmas brooding over Carly. What was the point of going over it again? *Of asking himself if he could have done more?*

He dressed quickly and walked down the corridor of the bustling maternity unit to his office, frowning when he saw the stack of paperwork on his desk. Picking up the first file, he sat down just as the door opened and Maggie slunk into the room, an anxious look on her face and a box of chocolates in her hand.

'These arrived from the woman we delivered yesterday. You'd better have one before they all go.' Scrutinising him closely, she closed the door behind her and walked across the room. 'Katherine has just gone to the ward. Paeds are happy with the baby which, by the way, is now named Patrick Gary.'

Reflecting on how his friend and colleague would greet that news, Patrick smiled. 'As long as it isn't Gary Patrick.'

Maggie rolled her eyes. 'You two are ridiculously competitive. I don't know how you managed to be in the mountain rescue team together and not push each other off a cliff.' She stuck the box of chocolates on his desk and sighed. 'All right. I'll come straight to the point. Are you OK? You didn't have to answer that woman's question about your wife. She's really worried she upset you. We're *all* worried about you.'

'She didn't upset me.' Patrick signed a document that had been left out for his attention. 'I'm fine, Maggie.' *And the last thing he wanted to talk about was his ex-wife.*

But Maggie showed no sign of shifting. 'I know you *hate* this time of year—have you heard from her? Has she been in touch?'

'No.' Resigned to having the conversation he didn't want to have, Patrick put his pen down. 'She sent a card and a cheque for me to choose something for the kids.' The anger rushed through him but he controlled it, as he always did. He'd trained himself to be civilised about the whole thing for the sake of the children. He didn't want them to feel like tennis balls being thumped between two players. 'She said I was more likely to know what they wanted than she was.'

Margaret's mouth tightened with disapproval and Patrick knew what she was thinking. The same thing he'd been thinking—*that Carly should have known exactly what to buy her own children for Christmas.*

'It's been two years since she walked out, Patrick. It's time you found someone else. Let's face it, it isn't going to be hard.'

Patrick gave a faint smile of mockery. 'Not hard at all to find someone you want to spend your life with and trust with your children's happiness.'

'All right, all right—it's hard.' Maggie pushed the box of chocolates towards him. 'The kids are lucky to have you. You're such an amazing dad.'

Patrick's jaw tensed. *If he was so amazing, why were his children living without their mother?*

'Maggie, I appreciate your concern but you don't need to worry about me. The children and I are fine. Goodness knows, my life is complicated enough without adding in a relationship.' He helped himself to a chocolate. 'Does this have nuts in it? I hate nuts. You midwives always know the chocolates by heart.'

'That's because we eat too many of them. That one's caramel. And relationships don't have to be complicated, Patrick.'

'Mine always seem to be.'

'That's because you picked the wrong woman last time. Next time choose a nice, kind motherly girl who would love those gorgeous children of yours and be proud to be with a high-flying doctor.'

'I don't want a nice, kind, motherly girl.' Patrick unwrapped the chocolate and ate it. 'I want a raving nymphomaniac with the gymnastic skills of an Olympic athlete.'

Margaret choked with laughter. 'And there was me thinking you need someone intelligent you can have a conversation with. I never knew you were so shallow. Or are you just trying to shock me?'

'I'm trying to shock you.' *And move her off the subject of his ex-wife.*

'What about that girl you met when you were in Chicago?'

Patrick sighed. 'Remind me why I told you about that?'

'I caught you in a weak moment.' Smiling,

Maggie settled herself on the edge of his desk. 'You *really* liked her, didn't you?'

'I spent twenty-four hours with her, Mags,' Patrick said carefully, pushing aside the memory of a girl with long legs and an endless smile— *and a night that would stay with him for ever.* 'Hardly a recipe for happy ever after.'

'You should have taken her number.'

'She didn't give me her number.' Patrick sat back in his chair, a wry smile on his face. 'Clearly she didn't want to repeat the experience.'

Maggie started to laugh. 'Is that really what you think? It's far more likely that she felt awkward at having spent the night with you and slunk out of your room before you woke up.'

Not having considered that possibility, Patrick frowned. 'She seemed pretty confident.'

'Was that before or after you'd removed her clothes?'

'Does it make a difference?'

'Of course it does! Confident women are often full of insecurities when they're naked. That's why we prefer to keep the lights off.'

They'd kept the lights on. *All night.*

'Enough!' Patrick aimed the chocolate wrapper

towards the bin in the corner of the room. 'You and I may have been colleagues for years but there are limits.'

'I'm just saying that maybe she didn't want you to see her in daylight.'

'She showed me around the hospital in daylight.'

'But presumably she was wearing clothes at that point.' Maggie dipped her hand into the box and pulled out a chocolate. 'Trust me, it's different. If I ever went to bed with you, I'd want the lights off.'

'If I ever went to bed with you, your husband would kill me.' Patrick emptied the contents of his in-tray into his briefcase. 'Can we drop this conversation? Relationships aren't a priority for me at the moment. And if you ever mention this to anyone else on the unit, I'll drown you in the birthing pool.'

Maggie looked smug. 'You really did like her.'

'Yes.' Exasperated, Patrick reached for his coat. 'Yes, I liked her. Satisfied?'

'You liked her a lot.'

'Yes, I liked her a lot.'

'Was she pretty?'

'Very.'

'Did she make you laugh?'

Patrick thought about the day they'd spent together. 'Yes. She was fun. She smiled all the time.' *Which had been a refreshing change after Carly's endless moaning.*

'And you didn't take her number?' Maggie rolled her eyes. 'I thought you were supposed to be clever.'

'Clever enough to spot when a relationship isn't going to work.' Patrick put his coat on. 'If she'd wanted me to have her details, she would have left her number. And even if she'd left her number, it would have been somewhere in Chicago because that's where she lives.' He snapped his briefcase shut. 'I, on the other hand, live in a small corner of England. Even if she hadn't made her feelings clear by slinking out of my bedroom, I wouldn't get in touch with her. It would never have worked and I don't need another romantic disaster.'

'So that's it, then?'

'That's it. It was just one night and the only reason you even know about it is because you have an uncanny ability to prise information from the innocent.'

'I care about you. You deserve to be with someone special.'

'My kids are special. I'm with them.' Patrick walked towards the door. 'Any luck finding an extra midwife willing to work over Christmas?'

'No. So far that particular miracle hasn't happened. I'm just hoping that no one has contractions on Christmas Day because there's definitely no room at this inn.'

'You can call me if you're desperate. I can always bring the children in with me. They can sit in the staffroom with the chocolates.'

'We'd love to see them. I haven't seen Posy for a few months. But I don't want to call you in over Christmas. You deserve the break.' Maggie walked to the door. 'I'm glad you didn't take the job in Chicago. I would have resigned and gone with you. Tell me honestly—were you tempted?'

Yes. Because if he'd taken the job, he would have seen the girl again.

He'd even picked up the phone once, but had put it down again before it could ring. What would he have said? *Hi, you know that night of hot sex we shared? Any chance you could give up your job and your life in the States and come and live over here so that we can do it again?*

Patrick sighed. He didn't even have to say it aloud to know it sounded ridiculous.

He'd already wrecked one woman's life. He wasn't going to do the same thing a second time.

'I wasn't tempted.' Reminding himself that he had two young children depending on him, he glanced at the clock. 'I'm off home. It's Christmas Eve tomorrow. I've promised to spend it with my children. This raving nymphomaniac you're finding me...' He gave Maggie a slow smile. 'Just make sure she has a passion for sexy underwear.' He regretted the words immediately.

She had worn the sexiest, classiest underwear he'd ever seen. Just thinking about the provocative silky knickers he'd found on the floor of his room the next morning made him glad he was wearing his coat.

'Go home and do battle with that turkey,' Maggie said cheerfully. 'I'll see you in three days.'

Discovering that there was nothing like the thought of cooking a turkey to cure a man of an attack of lust, Patrick groaned. 'I'd forgotten about the turkey. I'd rather deliver triplets than cook a turkey.'

Maggie gave a choked laugh. 'Welcome to the festive season. Merry Christmas, Patrick.'

'Merry Christmas.' Patrick felt exhausted as he thought of the challenge ahead of him. 'Yet another family Christmas that I'll mess up. Alfie still hasn't let me forget last year's turkey disaster. I need a miracle.'

CHAPTER ONE

HAYLEY climbed out of the taxi, slipped on the ice and landed hard on her bottom in the snow.

'Are you all right, love?' The taxi driver peered at her and she gave a weak smile as she slithered and slid her way back onto her feet, clutching the door for support and mentally itemising the damage.

'I'm fine,' she lied, trying not to picture the bruise that was going to appear later. 'Fortunately my bottom is big enough to provide a decent cushion. Which is useful because I'm not that great at walking on ice. Actually, I'm not that great at walking on pavements either. I'm the only person I know who can trip on a flat surface.'

The taxi driver chuckled sympathetically. 'Uncoordinated, are you? I have a sister like that. Always falling over, she is.' He flicked on the windscreen wipers to clear the snow. 'It's been great chatting to you, Hayley. Cheered up my Christmas Eve, you have. Feel as though I've known you for years.'

Remembering just how frank she'd been, Hayley squirmed with embarrassment. She'd said *far* too much. As usual. He knew everything about her except her bra size. Come to think of it, he probably knew that, too, because she *had* mentioned that she always felt nervous in strapless dresses. In her head she could hear her stepbrother's mocking voice saying, *Hayley doesn't have an 'off' switch.* But what was she supposed to do? She'd been in the car for twenty minutes and it would have been rude not to speak. 'I'm glad you were the one who picked me up from the station, Jack. And I hope you get that hip of yours sorted out soon.'

'I'm sure I will. The doctors are very clever around here. Good with their hands, you know?' He gave her a knowing wink and Hayley blushed, wondering what had possessed her to confess *that* particular bit of her life history.

'How much do I owe you, Jack?'

'Nothing. Haven't enjoyed a fare so much all year. You made me laugh so hard I almost had the

car off the road at that last corner,' he said cheerfully, setting his meter to zero. 'And if you really
want my opinion, I think your family should be
ashamed of themselves. If my daughter were a
midwife I'd be proud as punch—I wouldn't be
telling her she was wasting her talents and should
have been a lawyer. Where would the world be if
we all picked our jobs on the basis of how much
they pay? No wonder you wanted to come up
here and escape. Now, forget about the lot of them
and have a good time. I hope the romance works
out for you. With any luck he'll propose by New
Year and then you can invite me to your wedding.'

Wedding?

Had she actually confessed that bit of her
fantasy?

'If there's a wedding, you'll be there. I'll need
someone rooting for me on my side of the
church,' Hayley said weakly, holding onto the
door and wishing she hadn't revealed *quite* so
much to someone she'd known for twenty
minutes. It wasn't so bad to have told him why
she wasn't going home to her family for
Christmas, but it was probably a mistake to have
told him about *that night*.

But she was excited! And happy! And it was all because of a man.

At least now she was in the same country as him, she thought dreamily. The thought that he might be within miles of her made her want to sing and dance. It was only the knowledge that dancing might leave her with two broken ankles that stopped her from twirling in the snow.

That and the fact that she didn't want to make a bad impression on her new employer.

Brushing the snow from her coat, she thought to herself that for once—*just once*—it would be nice to be a naturally elegant and dignified person. She would have liked to arrive at her new job as housekeeper looking like one of those women you saw in magazines—long black coat, elegant boots, lipstick…

'You've got snow in your hair, love,' the taxi driver said helpfully, and then nodded at the house behind her. 'Well, this is it. High Fell Barn. Nice place. Smart. Like something from one of those fancy architect designed home programmes you see on the TV. I know you haven't met the family but I can tell you from looking at this that they're loaded. I wouldn't mind spending Christmas here myself. Starting to think you might be right to ditch the whole family thing.'

'Oh, no, I think family is wonderful,' Hayley said hastily, dragging snow out of her hair with her fingers. 'Just not *my* family. And they'd probably be all right if I was different. They're all scarily clever and co-ordinated and have really well-paid jobs and apartments with big windows and glass—you know the sort of thing. I was the runt of the litter. Well, actually I came from a different litter because they're my step-siblings. My mum married their dad and they never forgave me for that.' *She was doing it again, talking, talking, talking.* 'Anyway, enough of that,' she said lamely, and Jack smiled at her.

'Stepfamilies can be complicated. Everyone knows that. Lots of jealousy there.'

'I don't think my step-siblings are jealous,' Hayley said humbly. 'More embarrassed to be officially associated with me, I think.'

Whoops—here comes Hayley. How many babies has she dropped this year?

Not for the first time Hayley indulged in a swift fantasy about her acid-tongued stepbrother choking on a chicken bone and her saving his life with a skilfully performed Heimlich manoeuvre. Of course, he'd be blubbering with gratitude, her whole family open-mouthed with awe at her hidden talents, begging her forgiveness for having so grossly underestimated her.

We had no idea, Hayley.

Trying not to dwell on how inadequate her family made her feel, Hayley stared at the huge glass windows and the snow-covered roof of the barn. Despite the size of the place, it was the most welcoming building she'd ever seen. Lights twinkled along the front of the barn and through the window she could see a haphazardly decorated Christmas tree standing guard over piles of brightly wrapped parcels.

To the side of the barn was a wide stream in full flow, the winter silence disturbed by the roar and rush of white water as it frothed down from the top of the icy fells.

'That's the beck.' The taxi driver nodded. 'That's what we call it in these parts. In summer it's no more than a trickle of water but now, with the snow melting…'

'It's fantastic.' After the urban chaos of Chicago,

Hayley savoured the sound of the water smashing over the rocks on its way down the mountain.

Behind the barn stretched acres of fields, sparkling white with snow, and beyond that the forest and the mountains. Pine trees stood tall and straight as sentries either side of the barn, tiny twinkling lights twisted through their branches.

It was like something from a Christmas card. She half expected to see Santa and a team of reindeer hauling a large sack towards the gently smoking chimney.

'It's enough to lift your spirits, isn't it?' The taxi driver grinned at her. 'Talking of which, it's time I went home and lifted spirits with the wife. Brandy is her tipple. You never know—I might get lucky. Hope you do, too.'

'I don't know—I'm starting to think this might have been a mistake,' Hayley confessed, cautiously letting go of the car door and pushing her hands into her coat pockets for extra warmth. 'I don't even know where the guy lives. I just know it's the Lake District.'

'But you know he works at the hospital so he should be easy to track down once Christmas is over.'

Desperate for reassurance, she bit her lip. 'Do you think it's crazy to have come all this way to find a guy I've only met once?'

'I think it's brave.'

'Brave as in stupid or brave as in courageous?'

'If you hadn't done it, you would have spent the rest of your life thinking, What if he was the one? And what if he was? You'd have thrown it all away. What's the worst that can happen? He can reject you and you'll be a bit embarrassed. So what?'

Feeling her nerve seep out of her like air from a punctured tyre, Hayley decided that if she was going to find the courage to carry out this plan, she needed to end this conversation. 'Thanks for the lift, Jack. Merry Christmas.'

'Merry Christmas to you.' His eyes twinkled. 'Will you make it to the door without slipping?'

'Probably not, but don't worry—bruises suit me. I look good in blue and purple.' Hayley smoothed her hair, even though she knew that without a pair of straighteners and half an hour in front of a mirror her attempts to look groomed wouldn't make an impact.

With a final wave and toot of his horn, Jack drove away and Hayley was left staring at the house.

A pair of child's red Wellington boots were tipped over in the snow, and a tiny shovel had been discarded on the path, as if the owner hadn't been able to wait to run back inside this wonderful house and prepare for Christmas.

It wasn't a house, Hayley thought wistfully. It was a home.

A dream home.

And inside was a family who needed her—a family who wasn't going to spend the whole festive season treating her as the entertainment.

So why was she suddenly nervous?

Well, because she was always the same about decisions. Right thing, wrong thing? This or that? Invariably she jumped in with both feet and then realised that the other way was the better way. In fact, she'd spent most of her life unravelling the consequences of decisions she'd made.

When she'd been miles away in Chicago, Christmas with a bunch of strangers had seemed like a brilliant idea. Suddenly she wasn't so sure.

She was about to take a job with a family she'd never even met, in a part of the country she didn't know. And all so that she could avoid her own agonising family Christmas and track down a gorgeous stranger she'd spent one night with.

When she'd come up with the plan it had seemed bold and proactive.

A plan worthy of a competent, twenty-first-century woman.

Hayley swallowed. She didn't need her step-siblings to point out that she wasn't really a competent, twenty-first-century woman.

If she *were* a competent, twenty-first-century woman she wouldn't have slunk out of an impossibly sexy man's swanky hotel room before he'd woken up, neither would she have been wearing the previous night's dress and a scarlet face that announced her sins to anyone who happened to be looking. And she definitely wouldn't have left her knickers on his bedroom floor! A twenty-first-century woman would certainly have been able to find her knickers in the dark. Except that a twenty-first-century woman wouldn't have needed to. She would have woken up next to the impossibly sexy man, calmly ordered room service and then handed him her phone number or left with her head held high.

She had slunk out like a criminal, ensuring that there was no chance he would ever call her, because *he didn't have her number.*

All he had was her knickers.

At least Cinderella had had the sense to make it a shoe, Hayley thought gloomily as she picked her way through the snow to the front door. Losing a shoe made you seem slightly dippy and a little romantic—although it made it difficult to walk, of course. But losing knickers…

She didn't even want to think about how losing a pair of knickers made you look.

Prince Charming would never have roamed his kingdom looking for the bottom that fitted the knickers, would he?

Cross with herself, she kicked a lump of snow and watched it scatter. She'd met the man of her dreams *and then she'd walked out!* What an idiot. Her step-siblings would have laughed themselves sick. *Soppy, romantic Hayley, always dreaming of marriage and happy endings.*

Hayley sighed. She wasn't *that* old-fashioned. She *had* spent the night with him—although her embarrassingly quick surrender had had more to do with his superior seduction technique than her impressive decision-making abilities.

But she wasn't going to think about that now. She wasn't going to think about his skilled hands, or his clever mouth or the way he knew exactly where to touch and how...

Oh, God, please, please, don't let him reject her. Please let him be dreaming of her right now. And most of all please let him have spent the past few weeks frantically calling detective agencies trying to track her down. *All I know about her is that she has great taste in underwear.*

Surely he was going to be pleased to see her?

Imagining his reaction to her unexpected arrival brought a smile to her face. Perhaps she'd better make sure that their first meeting took place in private in case he just hauled her into his arms and proposed on the spot.

She wondered what her stepsister would say when she met him.

How did our Hayley ever get herself a man like that?

Smiling at her own fantasies, she reached towards the doorbell.

* * *

Patrick pushed the haphazardly wrapped presents under the tree and looked at his ten-year-old son. 'Alfie, why are you looking at the clock?'

Alfie gave a guilty start. 'I don't keep looking at the clock.'

'Yes, you do.'

'Well, it's Christmas Eve. I—I'm excited.' Alfie's gaze slid furtively to the door. 'Daddy, don't you wish you had someone to help cook the turkey?'

'I can cook a turkey.' Patrick added a strip of sticky tape to a parcel that was bursting out of its wrapping.

'Last year you said if you ever saw a turkey again it would be too soon.'

Patrick winced. *Was Christmas ever going to run smoothly?* 'That was last year. I've studied a cookery book. I don't foresee any complications.' He tried to look confident. He could perform a Caesarean section in less than four minutes if the need arose. Why did he struggle to cook a turkey?

'If you had a wife, she could cook the turkey.'

'That isn't a reason to get married. These days,

women don't always like doing that sort of thing.' Patrick extracted himself from under the tree, his wide shoulders dragging through the branches and sending a shower of needles over the pale wooden floor. 'Why are you talking about wives? We're going to have a great Christmas. You, Posy and me.'

'And the kittens.'

'And the kittens.' Remembering the kittens, Patrick frowned. 'That woman who phoned earlier is coming to look at them any moment now. With any luck she'll fall in love with them and that will solve one of our problems.'

'The kittens aren't a problem!'

'Having four of them is a problem.' Seeing the forlorn look on Alfie's face, Patrick felt a flash of guilt and squatted down in front of his son. 'Alfie, we cannot keep four kittens.'

Alfie fiddled with a bauble on the tree. 'What if the woman gets here and she doesn't want the kittens?'

'Why wouldn't she want the kittens? That's why she's coming.' Patrick scooped up a pile of discarded books and stood up. 'Take this lot up to your bedroom, will you? We need to make room for all the new mess you're going to make on Christmas Day.'

Alfie looked up at him, a flash of desperation in his eyes. 'Do you promise that whatever happens you won't be angry?'

Patrick frowned. 'Alfie, what is going on?' He forced himself to ask the question that always niggled at the back of his mind. 'Are you missing Mum? Is that what this is about?'

Alfie rubbed his foot along the groove in the floor. 'Do *you* miss her?'

How did you tell a child that divorce had come as a blessing?

'Your mum and I made a mistake when we got married,' Patrick said gruffly. 'It happens. It has nothing to do with you. We both love you.'

'But you didn't really love each other.'

Abandoning the books, Patrick squatted back down in front of his son. 'No,' he said quietly. 'We didn't. Not enough to make marriage work. We'd only known each other a month when we decided to get married.' He didn't add that Carly had become pregnant on purpose. 'We didn't know each other well enough and it's important to take the time to get to know someone. I didn't make your mum happy.'

'Is that why she was always yelling at you?'

'She didn't always yell,' Patrick said tactfully, but Alfie interrupted him.

'She yelled all the time. And that day she left— two Christmases ago—she shouted at you because you went to deliver those triplets when she had lunch on the table.'

Patrick knew from experience that there was no point in lying. 'That's right, she did. She was upset.'

'She said she was thinking of getting pregnant again because that way she might at least get to see you in the damn antenatal clinic.'

Patrick pressed his fingers into the bridge of his nose, knowing that this wasn't the time to lecture on language. He was just relieved that neither of his children appeared to have inherited his ex-wife's filthy temper. 'She was very angry with me,' he said evenly. 'She'd made plans for a special Christmas, but I was on call at the hospital and I—well, in my job, I can't always plan.' Not for a moment would he tell the child that his mother had liked the idea of being married to a wealthy obstetrician, but not the reality. 'Why are we talking about this now?'

'I don't know.' Alfie shrugged. 'Because it's Christmas and Mum left at Christmas.'

'Christmas can be a difficult time for lots of families,' Patrick said roughly, watching his son's face. 'Is it full of bad memories for you?'

'No. I like being with you,' Alfie said honestly. 'I like the fact that there's no shouting because you never shout. Does it make me bad that I don't miss her?'

Was that what had been worrying the child? *Guilt that he didn't miss his mother?* 'It doesn't make you bad.' Anger towards his ex-wife shot through him like white heat and Patrick hugged the boy tightly, feeling his heart split in two.

Alfie gave a croak of protest. 'Daddy, you're squeezing me!'

'Sorry.' His tone gruff, he released his hold. 'I love you. You know that, don't you?' The words came easily, driven by a burning determination to be a better father to his son than his own father had been to him. *To feel, and to express those feelings without embarrassment.*

'And I love you.' Alfie was openly affectionate. 'And you're the best doctor in the world, everyone says so. If you have to go to the hospital this Christmas, I'll come with you. We're a team. Team Buchannan. Do you think they'll have chocolates?'

Touched by the hero-worship, Patrick smiled. 'Stacks of them. Maggie is saving you the best. And, Alfie, I'm not the best doctor in the world.'

'You are. You're *so* cool. You saved Matt's little sister's life when she was born—she would have died if it hadn't been for you. And Jenna's mum says she'd marry you if you asked her.'

Startled, Patrick lifted his eyebrows. 'You heard her say that?'

'Yes. I heard her talking to another mum on the phone. She said you were really hot. But I don't see how she could have known what temperature you were because you weren't there and, anyway, it had just snowed. You made me wear a vest. How could you have been hot?'

Patrick let out a long breath and made a mental note to keep his distance from Jenna's mum. 'Well—I—'

'Do you want to get married again, Dad?'

Patrick felt the conversation spiralling out of control. 'Marriage is a big thing,' he said carefully, 'and when you've been wrong once, it makes you wary about doing it again. But maybe one day. If I know someone really, really well.' He wouldn't be making the same mistake he'd made with Carly. *No more whirlwind relationships.* Trying not to think about the girl he'd met in Chicago, he concentrated on his son. 'Do *you* want me to get married again?'

'It would be nice to have someone on our team who can cook.'

'I can cook.' Patrick picked up the books again. 'Just wait until tomorrow.'

Alfie looked unconvinced. 'Will you poison us? Uncle Daniel said the emergency department is always full on Christmas Day of people being poisoned with salmon—something, but I don't get how a turkey can turn into a fish.'

'Salmonella. It's a bacterium. And I'm not going to poison you.' Patrick dropped a kiss on his son's head. 'Time to wake Posy from her nap.' He lifted his head as the doorbell sounded. 'Ah—that will be the lady who wants the kittens.'

Alfie gulped and the guilt was suddenly back in his eyes. 'I'll get the door. You get Posy.'

Hayley stood on the doorstep, trying to look the way a competent housekeeper was supposed to look.

Fingering the advert in her pocket, she suddenly felt nervous. *Must like children and be able to cook turkey.* What exactly was this family expecting? A cross between Mary Poppins and a celebrity chef?

Thumps and childish shrieks came from behind the door and suddenly it was tugged open and a young boy stood there. There was a large blob of chocolate on his sweatshirt.

'Hi.' He gave her a tentative smile and then glanced nervously over his shoulder. 'You've come about the advert?'

'Yes.' Hayley took an instant liking to him. 'You must be Alfie. You look exactly the way you sounded on the phone.' Sweet, bright, bouncy, straightforward—nervous?

'I wasn't sure you'd come.'

Hayley wondered why he was nervous. Was he scared his new housekeeper was a dragon? 'I've been dying to meet you.' She gave him a friendly smile. 'I spoke to your dad briefly—is he in?'

The anxiety in the child's eyes bordered on panic. 'Yes. But there's something I need to—'

'Alfie?' A deep male voice came from behind him and a man strolled towards the door, a little girl in his arms. 'Is it the lady who rang about the advert?'

'Sort of.' Throwing Hayley a desperate look, Alfie shrank to one side and Hayley frowned slightly, disturbed that he seemed to be afraid of his father.

Hoping that she wasn't about to spend Christmas with a family even more dysfunctional than her own, she turned to introduce herself and gave a gasp of shock.

It was *him!*

Here. And every bit as good looking as she remembered in a rough, male I-can-kill-a-lion-with-my-bare-hands sort of way.

The smile started inside her and spread to her lips. What a fantastic coincidence! She wouldn't even have to take the trouble to track him down. He lived right here, in this beautiful barn with two beautiful children, and—

Her thoughts came crashing to a halt.

He lived with two beautiful children?

His two beautiful children?

Oh, God, he had children.

He wasn't an indecently handsome sex god, he was a faithless rat.

The shock was like a fist punching her hard in the stomach. Hayley gave a whimper of disbelief. Please let it be a mistake. *Please.* Don't let them be his children. Let him be looking after them for someone else.

No, no no…

But even as she stared in horror at her fantasy man, the little girl burrowed sleepily into his shoulder.

'Want to go back inside, Daddy,' she mumbled, and Hayley felt her happiness evaporate in an instant.

All that was left of her bright, shiny new life was the bitter, grey sludge of melted dreams.

So much for her fantasy man.

So much for imagining that he'd been thinking about her.

No wonder he hadn't contacted her.

He had another life. A family.

What now? How on earth was she going to get out of this mess she'd made for herself?

Hi, there, I came to find you but you're not the man I thought you were, so I'm going home now. And, by the way, I hope you trip and bash your head on something really hard.

A cold sweat of panic drenched her skin. What if his wife was in the house? Dear God, how was she going to face the woman? There was no way she'd ever threaten anyone's family.

Horrified, Hayley started to back away but her feet shot in different directions and she ended up flat on her back in the snow.

'Ow.' Pain mingled with humiliation as she stared up at the grey winter sky. And then she was being hauled to her feet—easily, as if she weighed nothing, the strength in his muscular grip making her feel light and feminine.

'Hayley?' His tone was guarded and his sexy blue eyes held a glimmer of disbelief. 'What are you doing?'

'Well, obviously it isn't that easy to walk in the snow,' she said defensively, and he frowned slightly.

'I meant—what are you doing *here?*' he said

gently, and Hayley realised that he hadn't yet worked out that she was the one who had answered his advert for a housekeeper.

What a nightmare.

How was he going to react when he discovered that his dirty little secret was supposed to be spending Christmas with them?

Looking at the two vulnerable children clinging to him, she felt a flicker of anger. It would serve him right to have a moment of panic. It might make him think twice before he did the same thing again.

He reached out a hand and touched her hair and all her violent thoughts faded away. Hayley gazed up at him for a moment, completely disorientated by his touch, oblivious to the snow that had managed to find its way inside her clothes. 'What are you doing?'

'Removing a pine cone from your hair.' He held up the small brown cone that was dusted with snow. 'I thought it might be uncomfortable.'

Nowhere near as uncomfortable as realising that your dream of the future had just crashed and burned.

'Dad? What's going on?' Alfie's puzzled

enquiry drew nothing more than a lift of an eyebrow from his father.

He showed no sign of guilt. His handsome face wasn't shifting into a sheepish look. He wasn't sending her silent messages. He was as relaxed as if he'd just opened the door to a carol singer.

Maybe he had affairs all the time. Maybe that was why he'd been so good at it—lots of practice.

The thought made her want to stuff a handful of freezing snow down the front of his trousers. She was sure that Diana, her stepsister, would have slapped his face at this point and then turned and stalked away. But Hayley had never hit anyone in her life and really effective stalking required good balance so that was out of the question.

But the thing that was really keeping her rooted to the spot were the two children hovering close to Patrick—*was that his name or had he lied about that, too?* It wasn't *their* fault that their father was fuelled by high-octane testosterone levels and a superstud sex drive. They shouldn't have to suffer. She wasn't going to be responsible for breaking two little hearts on Christmas Eve. And if he had any sort of decency he'd help her find a polite excuse and leave, otherwise she had a fairly good idea of what she was going to do with the carving knife and her plan didn't require a turkey.

'I told your dad my name on the phone.' Proud of her improvisation, she locked gazes with Patrick, giving him her best I-know-what-you're-up-to-but-I'm-not-going-to-drop-you-in-it-yet look but his features remained impassive.

She envied his composure. His face revealed nothing. Nothing. Not a glimmer. *Definitely not the sort of man who would reveal his bra size to a taxi driver.*

'You're the woman who phoned? It was you?'

'Yes.' And she was wondering why she hadn't recognised his voice. Presumably because she hadn't expected to hear it. It hadn't occurred to her that he had anything to do with the advert she'd answered.

The coincidence was ridiculously unfair.

It couldn't happen to anyone but her.

And now she had to work out a way to unravel the mess, but she couldn't concentrate on anything while he was staring at her. Those deep blue eyes made her mouth dry and her heart bumped against her chest. At one point during their fantasy night she'd even felt pleased that he'd left the light on because it had meant she could stare at him and marvel that such an indecently handsome man was in bed with *her.*

She should have known it was too good to be true.

Realising how naive she'd been, Hayley wanted to hide herself in a hole.

Why hadn't it occurred to her that he might be married?

She was stupid, stupid, stupid.

Of *course* a man as gorgeous as him was going to be married.

She'd chased all the way from Chicago to follow a dream that didn't even exist. It was too embarrassing for words.

For him it had just been a one-night stand. Hot sex. This was the twenty-first century—the divorce rate was higher than ever and people's priorities had changed. Her friends had short, meaningless relationships, didn't they? Some even boasted about it—as if the ability to have sex without feeling was something to be proud of. A sign of the times. Progression. People did it all the time.

Other people.

Not her. She was out of step. And that was the reason she was here, instead of just filing the night away in her memory.

Alfie was looking at her anxiously. 'You came because of the advert.'

'That's right.' And she'd been excited by the prospect of spending Christmas with a family other than hers.

'You answered the advert?' Patrick gave a faint frown, as if he found that surprising. Then he gave a little shrug. 'In that case, why are we all standing on the doorstep? Let's show you the kittens.'

'Kittens?' It was Hayley's turn to look confused. 'What kittens?'

'Our kittens. The kittens in the advert.' Patrick pushed the sleeves of his jumper up his forearms in a casual gesture that made her stomach curl with desire.

How could a man's arms be sexy? Those dark hairs were like a declaration of his masculinity. And why did he have to have such a good body? She'd spent an entire night exploring every muscular curve of his powerful physique.

Reminding herself that his wife probably did the same thing all the time, Hayley dragged her eyes away from his arms and his body and focused on the tumbled blonde curls of his daughter. His *daughter.* If looking at her didn't kill her libido, nothing would. He wasn't available. He'd never been available. Even for that one special night, he hadn't been hers.

'I don't know anything about kittens.' If he was making up some story to satisfy his son, she wished he'd at least make it plausible.

'You said you answered the advert,' he said patiently, and Hayley wondered why he was trying to make her look stupid.

'I did. The advert asked for a live-in housekeeper over Christmas. Someone to cook a turkey.'

'I didn't advertise for a housekeeper.'

'I spoke to you a few hours ago.' *How could a man look so good dressed in faded jeans and a black jumper?* 'I asked you about the children. You told me that you had two—a boy and a girl.' He'd look good in anything, she decided. And nothing.

His eyes were narrow and assessing. 'We were talking about the kittens,' he breathed. 'We have kittens that need a good home. A boy and a girl— which is what I put in the advert. No mention of a housekeeper. Nothing about turkeys.'

He was going to pretend he didn't know?

Hayley dug in her pocket and pulled out the crumpled advert. 'Here.' She pushed it into his hand, noticing that the little girl had inherited her father's killer blue eyes. '*Someone who knows how to cook a turkey*—that's what it says.'

'Can I see that?' His fingers brushed against hers and that touch was sufficient to ignite the same powerful chemistry that had made her forget morals, common sense and her own rules and spend the night with a stranger.

Determined to look as indifferent as he did, Hayley yanked her hand away and pushed it into the pocket of her coat. If her hands were in her coat then she couldn't give way to the temptation and touch him, could she?

'I don't know anything about this advert.' He scanned it swiftly, a puzzled frown on his face. 'It's our phone number, but—' His voice tailed off and he slowly turned his head and looked at his son, his blue eyes suddenly dark with suspicion. 'Is this the reason you've been so jumpy all day?'

Pinned by his father's sharp, questioning gaze, Alfie shrank against the door. 'I can explain…'

Patrick was ominously still. 'I'm waiting.'

Alfie fiddled with his sweatshirt and gave an audible gulp. 'Uncle Dan was placing that advert for the kittens when you were away having that interview in Chicago and he was looking after us. He kept saying, "Problem solved," and I thought if we got ourselves a housekeeper, that would be another problem solved.'

'Are you saying that Uncle Daniel placed this advert for a housekeeper?'

Alfie stared up at his father in silence, apparently frozen to the spot. 'No.' His denial was a tiny squeak. 'That was me. I did it. It wasn't Uncle Dan.'

Hayley wondered why the child's mother couldn't cook the turkey. Was she hopeless in the kitchen? Or maybe super-stud kept her too busy in the bedroom, she thought miserably. Or perhaps his wife thought cooking was beneath her, like her stepsister did.

Hayley watched as Patrick gradually coaxed the truth from his son. She sensed that he was angry—he *had* to be angry—and she braced herself for him to yell.

Suddenly she couldn't bear it.

The little boy was so sweet, he didn't deserve

to be yelled at by a father who couldn't keep his trousers zipped.

But Patrick didn't yell. Instead, he hunkered down in front of his son. 'You advertised for a housekeeper over Christmas?'

'We need someone, Dad,' the boy blurted out. 'You're good with babies, but you're hopeless with turkeys. And the rest of the Christmas stuff. And you're bound to be called to the hospital because you always are and then you'll call Mrs Thornton—and I *hate* Mrs Thornton. Her lips are too red. It's like she's drunk *blood* or something.' The child glanced at Hayley and she gave a sympathetic shrug.

'That can happen with red lipstick,' she muttered. 'You have to be really careful with the shade. I once had one that made me look as though I'd been punched in the face. Hopeless.'

Alfie gave a delighted laugh while Patrick looked at her with incredulous disbelief.

Hayley stiffened defensively. 'What?' She was fed up with him looking at her as though she was from another planet. 'I happen to agree with Alfie. Red is a very dodgy shade. And, anyway, whoever wears red lipstick for babysitting?'

'She wears it because she fancies my dad,' Alfie told her, and Hayley rolled her eyes.

Another one?

The man was even having sex with the baby-sitter. Had he no shame?

'Can we get back to the subject?' His voice slightly tighter than it had been a few moments earlier, Patrick ran his hand over the back of his neck and turned his attention back to his son.

'Where did you get the money for the advert?'

He would have made a good interrogator, Hayley thought moodily, remembering how much information she'd given him during their day and night together. Every time he'd looked at her with those sexy blue eyes, she'd divulged another personal detail.

Alfie's face was scarlet. It was obvious that he *hated* being in the wrong.

Hayley knew that feeling.

'Uncle Dan left his credit card by the phone,' the child mumbled, and Patrick's mouth tightened.

'And you took it?'

'If he was careless enough to leave it lying around then he can't complain if it was abused,' Hayley said firmly, glaring at Patrick as he sent her a slow, fulminating look. Really, he was hardly in a position to be self-righteous, was he?

He turned back to Alfie, who was gazing at Hayley as though she were a lifebelt and his father was a giant wave. 'I'll pay him back, Dad. I promise. I'll clear snow or something and earn some money.'

'How could you place an advert? Didn't the newspaper know you were a child?'

'They asked me how old I was and I made a joke of it. I said my dad had no idea how to cook a turkey and I needed an expert.'

'So if she rightly insisted on checking with a grown-up, how did this advert...' Patrick waved the cutting slowly '...end up in the paper?'

'Uncle Daniel walked back into the room and I told him he needed to just say that the advert was all fine.' Alfie swallowed. 'And he did that. He wasn't concentrating. Posy was coughing really badly. He thought he was confirming the kitten advert.'

Patrick scanned the crumpled, torn newspaper in his hand. 'Instead of which he confirmed an advert for a housekeeper to come and spend Christmas with us.'

'I thought if it worked out all right, you'd be pleased,' Alfie confessed in a small voice. 'And then when I woke up today, I wasn't so sure. I thought you might be angry. Are you really angry, Dad?' Alfie looked so forlorn that Hayley's spine stiffened at the injustice of it.

Poor Alfie.

She glared at the back of Patrick's head, determined not to notice his cropped dark hair. Who cared if he looked macho? And good shoulders weren't everything, were they? He was a snake. How *dared* he give his son that you've-disappointed-me-with-your-behaviour look, while betraying his marriage vows in every empty bed he could find, *and* with a woman who had no taste in lipstick.

Hayley was about to leap passionately to Alfie's defence when Patrick tugged the boy into his arms.

'How can I be angry when it's my fault for being so lousy at cooking Christmas dinner?' His tone gruff, he released his son and ruffled his hair. 'I like the fact you saw a problem and tried to solve it. And I'm proud that you used your initiative.' He spoke quietly, keeping the conversation between him and his son. 'I also like the fact that you've been honest with me and not tried to duck out of it. But it *was* wrong of you to use Uncle Daniel's credit card, Alfie. That was stealing. We'll need to talk about that later.'

Hayley subsided slightly, although she was still simmering at his devoted dad act. Devoted dads didn't take advantage of their sex appeal, did they? Devoted dads weren't supposed to turn into sex gods in their spare time.

Patrick straightened and looked her directly in the eye and Hayley glared back, hoping he couldn't read her mind and wishing she could look as cool and unflustered as he did.

'There's been a mistake.' As his eyes flickered to her mouth she wondered exactly which mistake he was referring to—the advert, or the night they'd spent together.

'I can see that. You obviously don't want a housekeeper so I'll leave you to cook your own turkey and I hope you find a good home for the kittens.' Trying to maintain her dignity, she picked up her bags and smiled at Alfie. 'You have a lovely Christmas. I hope Santa brings you everything you want.'

Proud of the way she'd handled herself so far,

Hayley knew that what she needed to do next was turn and walk away, but walking on snow hadn't been a great success so far, had it? And, anyway, where was she supposed to walk to? They were in the middle of the countryside with snow-capped mountains behind them and the stream in full flood only a few steps away. If she stalked off here, her body would be discovered frozen in the morning encased in a layer of ice and very possibly washed into the next valley. And dignity and hypothermia were definitely incompatible. 'Go back inside. It's freezing. I'll call a taxi.' *Hopefully before his wife emerged to see what was going on.*

At least he didn't know she'd come here specifically to see *him.*

That was one small consolation.

'You can't go!' Alfie sounded horrified. 'And we *do* need a housekeeper. Dad can't cook a turkey, honestly. And if you leave, you won't be able to surprise your friend. Remember? You told me that on the phone. You said you were coming over to surprise a special friend and you needed somewhere to live while you tracked him down.'

Oh, no. No, no, no.

Feeling Patrick's gaze on her face, Hayley wanted to throw herself into the stream. Her impetuous nature had got her into some embarrassing situations in the past, but none quite so embarrassing as this one.

It was almost as bad as that day at school when she'd discovered that her stepbrother had planted a camera in the girls' showers.

All she needed now was for Patrick to produce her knickers from his pocket and her humiliation would be complete.

He leaned against the doorframe, watching her. 'You came here to look for...someone?' His pause was significant and Hayley felt her face fire up to a shade that probably matched the dreadful Mrs Thornton's vampire lipstick.

How dared he look amused? *Obviously* he was a sadist as well as being hugely insensitive. And an adulterer. This situation was about as amusing as discovering you were the only one in fancy dress and everyone else was in black tie. As the list of his crimes grew longer, Hayley grew more affronted.

'I'm not looking for anyone. I mean—I might have been, originally, yes...' She knew she was babbling incoherently, but all hope of a smooth response had deserted her. 'My friend let me down.' She looked at him pointedly and saw his eyes narrow slightly. 'So I won't be looking for him.'

'Is that right?' His soft drawl was as annoying as his blank expression and Hayley wondered whether falling face down in the snow would put out the fire in her cheeks.

Deciding that she needed to make her exit no matter how undignified, Hayley started to back away but Alfie grabbed her arm.

'No, I won't let you go! Dad, tell her she has to stay! I know you didn't put the advert in, but she's here now and think how great it would be to have someone helping over Christmas. Dad? *Say* something.'

CHAPTER TWO

SHE had the sexiest mouth he'd ever kissed.

Not beautiful—her mouth was too wide to qualify for beautiful—but soft, full and with a slight pout that made a man think the most basic, primitive thoughts. And then there was the tiny dimple in the corner that was so deliciously feminine. Suddenly Patrick wished life wasn't so complicated. All he wanted to do was throw her over his shoulder and carry her up to his bed.

The fact that she was flustered, embarrassed and visibly angry with him did nothing to cool his libido. Far from it. It just reminded him how refreshingly open she was with people. He'd seen that from the first moment they'd met—been intrigued by just how much she'd divulged about herself as she'd shown him around the hospital.

He even found her slightly ungainly battle with the ice appealing. The fact that she didn't seem fully in control of her legs simply reminded him that she had incredible legs. Incredibly *long* legs.

A vivid image of exactly how long her legs were brought a groan to his lips but he managed to stifle it. Why did everything about her make him think of sex?

He remembered the moment when she'd landed flat on her back in the snow. For an unsettling moment, the contrast between her dark hair and the white powder had reminded him of how she'd looked against the sheets in his hotel room and he'd been on the verge of lowering himself on top of her and doing what he was burning to do when Alfie had disturbed his red-hot daydream.

And now his son was looking at him, waiting for an answer.

Dragging his mind away from sex, Patrick tried to remember the question.

But what did you say to a woman with whom you'd been intimate but hadn't expected to see again?

Hi, there—what are you doing on my doorstep?

Patrick stood in silence, the reality of his life

squashing the fantasy. He felt the children looking at him and he knew that, no matter what he said next, someone was going to be hurt. If he told her that they didn't need a housekeeper then she'd be hurt and so would Alfie. If she stayed—

He dismissed the thought impatiently.

How could she possibly stay?

They always said that the past would catch up with you, but he hadn't expected it to catch up with him this quickly—*hadn't thought his children would find out about what had happened in Chicago.*

On the other hand, there had to be a reason why she was here. And only one reason came to mind.

She was pregnant.

She *had* to be pregnant. It was the only explanation for the fact that she was standing on his doorstep on Christmas Eve. She'd travelled over six thousand miles to talk to him.

Patrick closed his eyes briefly, forcing himself to stay calm and think clearly.

He still didn't understand how her visit to the UK had somehow become entangled with Alfie's innocent advert for a housekeeper. All he knew was that his private moment of self-indulgence was no longer private. And the fact that she was pregnant...

Biting back a word he tried never to say in front of his children, Patrick ran his hand over the back of his neck and concentrated on her face. If he looked at his kids he'd just feel guilty and lose his thread, and that wasn't going to help anyone.

They were going to be hurt. That was inevitable.

It was up to him to try and minimise the damage.

'Dad?' Alfie was throwing strange looks at him. 'Say something. She can cook, Dad,' he urged. 'I know she's a stranger, but why wouldn't you want her to stay?'

Because she wasn't a stranger.

But he wasn't ready to confess as much to Alfie. Not yet. Not until he'd worked out the best way of handling the situation. For now he needed to pretend that this was the first time he'd met her.

Patrick's eyes lingered on her long, dark hair. It was damp from the snow and curled softly over her shoulders, the rich colour emphasising the pallor of her skin.

Her eyes met his briefly and then she turned to Alfie.

'Don't worry.' Despite her obvious agitation,

she gave the child a soft, reassuring smile. 'I can see there's been a mix-up.'

The icy wind blew a flurry of snow around her ankles and Patrick noticed that the bottoms of her jeans were as wet as her coat.

'You're wet—shivering.' The doctor in him suddenly felt concern but she shrugged it off.

'I'm fine.' Avoiding his gaze, she dug her hand into her pocket and pulled out a shiny pink phone. 'Go back in the warm. I'm sorry I can't help you out with those kittens. I'll just call a cab and I'll be out of your way.'

She thought he was just going to let her go?

Did she think he was the sort of man who would let a pregnant woman walk away in the depth of winter?

Feeling the familiar weight of responsibility, Patrick decided that the first thing he needed to do was get her inside quickly, before she became any colder.

Hypothermia wasn't a good state for anyone, let alone a pregnant woman.

'Dad?' Alfie nudged him. 'It's really bad manners to keep someone on the doorstep! You taught me that.'

'Yes. Hayley, please come inside.' Without giving her the opportunity to object, he stepped forward and picked up her small suitcase. 'We can talk about it in the warm. It's freezing out here and it's snowing again. And you're wet.'

'I'm only a little damp.' Her teeth were chattering. 'Nothing that won't dry.'

'Nothing is going to dry out here.' He watched with mounting exasperation as fresh snowflakes settled on her hair. 'Come in. Please.' He could see her backing off and his mouth tightened. Doubtless, now that the moment was here, she was dreading having to tell him her news.

'I'll call a taxi.'

'Hayley, it's Christmas Eve. You're in the Lake District, not London. There won't be that many taxis around, and they won't be driving out here.'

'Jack only dropped me twenty minutes ago. I'm sure he'll be happy to turn round and pick me up again.'

'Jack?' Her suitcase still in his hand, Patrick frowned. 'Who is Jack?'

'The taxi driver.'

'You're on first-name terms with the taxi driver?'

'He was a nice guy.'

'Right.' He'd forgotten how friendly she was. And yet hadn't it been her warmth and humanity that had attracted him to her that day at the hospital in Chicago? She'd had a smile and a greeting for every person they'd passed. 'Well, Jack has probably gone home to his family by now. Come inside, at least while we decide what to do.'

He didn't blame her for being wary of him. He'd hardly given her a warm welcome, had he?

'Please.' Alfie slipped his hand into hers. 'Come and see my kittens. And I can show you the presents under the tree.'

Hayley murmured another refusal but Alfie gave her hand a determined tug and she stepped over the threshold of the barn, as cautious as a deer sensing danger. 'Just for a moment. Then I'm calling a cab.'

Patrick put her cases down and closed the door on the cold. 'I'll make a hot drink while we decide what to do. Tea? Coffee? Hot chocolate?' *Was she nauseous? No, she couldn't possibly be nauseous. It was too early.*

'Tea, please.' Her tone was polite and she seemed to be making a point of not looking at him. 'Tea was the thing I missed most. It just doesn't taste the same in America.'

'You've come from America?' Alfie's eyes were round. 'My dad went to America a few weeks ago. He had an interview for a job, but he didn't like it.'

Patrick closed his eyes briefly. This was her chance to drop him in it but she merely smiled at Alfie, her cheeks dimpling prettily.

'Is that right? Well, you live in a beautiful place and I can quite see why he wouldn't want to leave it. After all, he has family here.' Her eyes slid to Patrick's and he saw the accusation in her gaze. 'A lovely family.'

Alfie opened the cake tin and helped himself to a brownie, oblivious to the sudden tension between the two adults. 'Are you American?'

'No.' Her smile didn't slip. 'I'm English.'

'Then why were you working in America?'

Her hesitation was so brief it was barely noticeable. 'I wanted a change. A fresh start. So a year ago I took a job there.'

'Why did you need a change?'

'Alfie!' Patrick's tone was sharp and he turned away to fill the kettle, still trying to work out how he was going to engineer privacy so that they could have the necessary grown-up conversation. 'It's rude to ask so many questions.'

'It's all right. I'm not big on secrets.' Her swift, pointed glance in his direction was another accusation. 'I wanted to do something completely different, Alfie, to prove to myself that I could. Sometimes when people have knocked your confidence, you start to see yourself the way they see you. Then it's good to get away from everyone and see what you can do when you haven't got people waiting for you to make a mistake.'

'Someone was waiting for you to make a mistake?' Alfie's horrified expression reflected Patrick's own thoughts.

'Who?' He barked the question angrily and then saw Alfie's startled look and frowned. 'What?'

'Dad, you look *really* mad.'

'I'm not mad,' he lied. 'I just…' He gestured with his hand. 'I mean, Alfie and I would both—we'd like to know who undermined your confidence.'

Hayley was looking at him as if he was slightly mad and he didn't blame her. The strength of his reaction had shocked him, too.

'That doesn't really matter,' she said faintly, turning her attention back to Alfie. 'Anyway, as I was saying, I wanted to prove myself so I took a job in this big, fantastic hospital in Chicago.'

Alfie nodded. 'I've seen Chicago on television.'

'Right. Well, I'd never even been to America before. I didn't know anyone and at first it was hard—strange...' She frowned slightly. 'But then I settled down and it felt good. I love midwifery.'

'You're a midwife?' Alfie gave a gasp. 'Dad, did you hear that? Hayley is a midwife!'

Patrick ran his hand over the back of his neck. Alfie was a bright boy and any moment now he was going to put two and two together. And there was absolutely nothing wrong with his son's maths. 'That's...great.'

'My Dad's an obstetrician,' Alfie said proudly. 'You guys can talk about babies if you like. I don't mind.'

Patrick winced. He had a feeling that the subject of babies was going to be right at the top of their list of conversation topics.

What were her plans?

Was she upset about being pregnant?

Was that why she kept sending him angry looks?

'Tell her she has to stay, Dad.'

Patrick made two mugs of tea. *If she was pregnant then she'd be staying a long time.* Was that what she wanted? Was that what *he* wanted?

No. Definitely not. A baby was *not* a reason to get married. He'd learned that the hard way. There were other ways of being responsible. 'Hayley and I need to talk in private, Alfie.' He decided that there was no point in postponing the inevitable. 'I'd like you to take Posy and go and watch a cartoon or something.'

'I've seen all the cartoons on television.' Alfie didn't budge. 'It's Christmas Eve. And Hayley doesn't have anywhere else to go because she thought she was going to be living here. We've got plenty of space—I don't understand why you want her to go.'

Because he felt suffocated, trapped—back in the same place he'd been before. Patrick looked at his son—*the son he was going to hurt*—his mind already racing forward, planning how he was going to break the news that there was going to be another child in their family. 'It's complicated, Alfie.'

'You're making me feel bad because this is all

my fault!' The child's eyes shone with tears. 'I didn't know it was going to turn out like this. I thought you'd be really grateful that you didn't have to cook the turkey by yourself. I was just trying to help!' Bursting into tears, he stormed out of the room and Posy ran after him, trailing her velvet comforter behind her.

Hayley made a distressed sound. 'Go after him.' Troubled, she turned to Patrick. 'Just go after him. I'll call myself a taxi and sort something out. I shouldn't have come.' Her phone was in her hand again and Patrick walked over to her.

'Wait—put the phone away, Hayley...' The scent of her hair wound itself around his senses and his eyes dropped to her mouth, everything he'd been intending to say evaporating from his mind. A rush of heat poured through his body and he knew he had to get to the point before he did something that complicated matters even further. 'Tell me why you're here.'

'Because everyone does stupid things at least once in their life and this was my moment,' she muttered. 'Don't worry about it. Go to your child, Patrick.'

Don't worry about it?

'Alfie will be all right for a minute,' he said roughly. 'We have things to talk about.' Even while his brain was warning him that this was a *big* mistake, his body was reacting to her presence. He wanted to slide his hands into her damp, silky hair—*he wanted to press his mouth to those rosy lips.*

Reminding himself that those impulses were the reason he was in his current mess, Patrick ruthlessly reined in his baser instincts. 'You came over here to see me, and… I know it's difficult, but just tell me the truth. Tell me whatever it is you came to tell me.'

She must be dreading telling him—afraid of his reaction.

And he braced himself not to overreact, reminding himself that this must have been hard for her. *She must be worried sick.*

But even while he was acknowledging her emotions, he was even more acutely aware of his own. He was angry with himself. And frustrated. And fiercely determined that this time he was going to do the right thing. And that was not going to include marriage.

'I didn't come here to tell you anything. I just

thought it was time for a change and I might as well...' Her voice tailed off and she blushed scarlet. 'All right, yes. I came to find you. Could you stop looking at me like that? This is embarrassing enough without you studying me as though you're a prosecution lawyer or something.' Her whole body was shivering and Patrick sighed and grabbed his heavy coat from the back of the door. He peeled off her damp coat in a decisive movement and placed the dry one around her shoulders. It swamped her, of course, because she was so much smaller than he was, and that evidence of her vulnerability pricked his conscience.

'I understand that this is difficult—' he fought back the urge to just demand the truth '—but you obviously have something to say to me and I really think it would be better for both of us if you just came right out and said it.'

He wanted to know what he was dealing with. They needed to talk dates, make plans—preferably before his children lost interest in television.

'All right. I'll say it.' She looked up at him, her dark hair falling in damp curls over his coat, a spark in her eyes. 'I think you're quite possibly the biggest snake and the most *horribly* insensitive man I've ever met.

Stunned, Patrick stared at her. 'Sorry?'

'I said you're a snake. And horribly insensitive. And you're a hypocrite, of course.' She seemed to gain confidence as she talked. 'And two-faced because you're pretending to be such a great father but you're obviously sleeping with every woman who takes your fancy even if her lipstick is hideous, which means you also don't have much taste and that makes it even worse—'

'Hayley—'

'And you may be seriously good-looking and have a fit body—a very fit body, actually…' her eyes slid to his shoulders before she looked away quickly '…and be super-intelligent, and obviously quite staggeringly talented in bed, but that doesn't mean you can just abandon morals and common decency and—'

'Hayley—'

'And I don't think a rampant sex drive is an excuse, and the worse thing is you're a liar because you didn't *once* mention your children or the fact that you're married, and—'

'Hayley, I'm divorced.'

'If you really didn't—' She broke off and stared at him. 'What did you say?'

'I'm divorced.' Patrick spoke the words quietly. 'My wife and I separated two years ago. I haven't seen her since then. And you need to breathe before you pass out.'

'You— I...' Her voice cracked. 'You're *divorced?*'

'Yes.'

'Well, why didn't you say so? Why didn't you tell me that night?'

'It didn't seem relevant.'

Hayley rolled her eyes. 'Only a *man* would think that wasn't relevant. Of *course* it's relevant! What about your children? Did you forget about them, or were they irrelevant too?'

'My children had nothing to do with the night we spent together.'

Her mouth fell open. 'You see? That's what I mean. You come across as this really caring guy—a bit macho perhaps, but basically caring—and then you go and deny your children!'

'I'm not denying my children,' Patrick said patiently. 'I'm saying they had no relevance to the night we spent together.'

'You mean you conveniently forgot them.' Her breathing rapid, she stroked her hair away from her face. 'Well, at least you're divorced. That's one thing to be grateful for.' Realising what she'd said, she blushed scarlet and shrank slightly. 'Sorry, sorry. That came out wrong. What I meant to say was—*obviously* it's not good that you're divorced, but I'm relieved to know you're not married.'

Patrick stilled, his radar on full alert and screaming a warning. 'Why would you be relieved?' His tone was several shades cooler as he contemplated the gulf between her expectations and his. 'Because now you know I'm available?'

She looked at him as though he was mentally incapacitated. 'No. Because I don't have affairs with married men, of course.'

'Right. Of course.' She sounded so affronted that he wanted to smile, and it occurred to him that this woman continually surprised him. He was trying to adjust his expectations when he realised that she was glaring at him.

'Are you laughing at me?'

'Absolutely not.'

'Good, because I don't see anything to laugh about.'

'Me neither.' Reminded of the reason she was here, Patrick's desire to smile faded instantly. 'Can I talk now?'

She stood stiffly. 'Of course. Go ahead.'

Patrick rested his hips against the kitchen table, wishing he could switch off the urge to take her straight to bed. 'First—I'm sorry if I was insensitive. It was a shock to see you on the doorstep and I accept that I probably didn't handle that as well as I could have done.'

'If you'd—'

He leaned forwards and pressed his fingers against her lips. 'It's my turn to talk, Hayley,' he drawled softly, watching as her eyes widened. Her lips softened and parted against his fingers and he removed his hand, wishing he'd found some other less erotic way of silencing her. 'Let me finish.'

The tip of her tongue traced her lips where his fingers had been a moment before and it took Patrick a moment to remember what he'd been planning to say.

'I'm not a hypocrite. I try and be a good father, although I'm sure I fall short of that ambition fairly frequently, and, despite the evidence to the contrary, which I admit in your case is incontrovertible, I am not sleeping with every woman who crosses my path. And while I'm flattered that you think I'm good-looking and you like my body—'

'I didn't exactly mean to say that bit out loud,' she muttered, and Patrick gave a faint smile and continued.

'I can assure you that I have not abandoned morals and common decency.' He watched as her smooth cheeks turned a delicious shade of pink. 'Neither have I ever lied to you.'

'Maybe not directly. But you didn't mention your children.' She looked tired, disillusioned and younger than he remembered, and for some reason she reminded Patrick of the young single mothers he sometimes saw in the antenatal clinic. Occasionally they were excited, but often they were overwhelmed and daunted by the enormity of it all.

He felt a twinge of guilt.

She was probably worrying about being alone and pregnant and she had no idea how to bring up the subject.

Instinctively he took charge of the situation.

'Hayley, I didn't mention the children

because we had other things on our minds. Which brings us neatly to the reason for your visit.' Deciding to make it as easy as possible for her, he turned briefly to make sure the kitchen door was shut. 'I'm sure you're feeling really mixed up about the whole thing. I'm sure it's come as a shock. I'm sure you're scared.' *Were there any other emotions he'd missed?* She'd called him insensitive and he was doing his best to be as sensitive as possible. 'But I don't want you to be scared. I take full responsibility. It was my fault. To be honest, I don't understand how it happened because I thought I'd protected you, but we'll work something out, I promise you that. You're not on your own.'

'Protected me?'

In the circumstances he couldn't blame her for sounding stunned. He *hadn't* protected her, had he? Clearly something had failed that night. And she blamed him. She had every right to be angry.

'As I said, I take full responsibility. But we need to talk about this calmly. We need to work out a solution together.'

'What are you taking responsibility for? It

was my decision to come here. You had nothing to do with it.'

'But I'm glad you came.'

'Are you?' Her voice faltered and she looked at him carefully. '*Really? I thought I'd made things awkward for you by coming.*'

'Well, obviously it's a shock.' He wasn't going to tell her just how much of a shock. She obviously needed reassurance that he wasn't going to overreact. 'But we'll work something out. Let's start with the practicalities. You're sure you're pregnant? It's pretty early on. There's no mistake about that?'

'*Pregnant?*' The word seemed to echo around the kitchen and Patrick winced, hoping that Alfie wasn't listening outside the door.

'Hayley, could you please try not to—?'

'You think I'm *pregnant!*' She backed away from him, so agitated that her breath came in uneven jerks. 'Is that why you think I'm here? Because I'm pregnant?'

How many times did she have to say the word?

'Yes, of course. Why else…?' His voice tailed off as he registered the shock on her face.

'*Why would you think I was pregnant?*' Her

tone made it obvious that he'd made the wrong assumption and Patrick pressed his fingers to the bridge of his nose, wishing he'd broached the subject differently.

'It was a shock to see you on my doorstep. I just assumed—'

'I didn't know it was your doorstep! And what did you assume? That the only reason I'd come to find you is because I was *pregnant?*' She made a distressed sound and started to pace around his kitchen, breathing so rapidly that Patrick eyed her with concern.

'You're hyperventilating, Hayley, and—'

'I am *not* hyperventilating,' she gasped, her hand pressed to her chest. 'I'm trying to control my emotions. It's all down to the breathing.'

'Right.' He watched her carefully, sure that she must be making herself dizzy. 'But you're breathing a bit fast. I'm a doctor, and I can see that you—'

'Oh, shut up, Patrick!' She groaned his name and turned away, digging her fingers into her hair and shaking her head in disbelief. Then she took a long deep breath and let her hands drop, as if she'd come to a decision. 'All right, I'm going to make a really big effort to think the way you seem to think. So—the sequence of events goes like this. Boy meets girl, boy sleeps with girl who conveniently lives in a foreign country so boy is never going to see her again, girl turns up on doorstep—girl must be pregnant.' She looked at him. 'That's what you're thinking?'

Given that that was *exactly* what he was thinking, Patrick didn't utter a denial and she made a faint sound in her throat.

'So, still thinking like you—although I have to confess that's a challenge—presumably the next demand I'm going to make is for money, is that right? Or marriage. Oh, God, *now* I understand your remark about married men being unable to give me what I want. Is that why you think I'm here? Because I'm looking for a *meal ticket?* God, that's truly awful.' She plopped back down on the nearest chair, as if her legs couldn't be trusted to hold her. 'You'd get on really well with my stepbrothers. They think life is all about money and using people, too.'

Feeling the situation spinning out of control, Patrick intervened. 'Judging from your reaction, I assume I'm wrong.'

Her breathing still far too rapid, she stared sight-lessly at a spot on his kitchen floor. 'Yes,' she snapped. 'You're wrong. Of *course* you're wrong. I haven't even missed a period, for goodness' sake.' She broke off, her face scarlet, and Patrick sighed.

'You don't have to be embarrassed,' he said quietly. 'I'm an obstetrician.'

'I know you're an obstetrician!' She squirmed in her seat, the look she flung him suggesting she wished he was in a different profession. 'Is that why your mind went off on that track? Because you're obsessed with babies?'

He took a deep breath, thinking of what had happened with Carly. 'It just seemed…possible. But obviously I was wrong.'

'Yes. You're wrong. And so was I. About a lot of things.'

He wasn't sure he wanted to explore that final cryptic remark, sensing that he might find the trans-lation more than a little uncomfortable to hear.

The fact that she *wasn't* pregnant should have filled him with relief but instead he felt nothing but concern. She looked shocked and *horribly* pale and the bulk of his coat made her seem even more fragile.

Patrick suddenly realised that this was the first time he'd seen her without a smile on her face. In the short time they'd spent together, she'd smiled constantly. In fact, it had been her warm, engaging smile that had attracted him to her in the first place. He'd wanted to press his mouth to that smile and taste the happiness she exuded.

But her smile had gone and he knew that he was the reason the light had gone out inside her. She was right. He *was* insensitive.

'Hayley—I owe you an apology.' He tried to redeem himself. 'Can we start this conversation again?'

'I don't think so. It was bad enough the first time.' She gave a tiny, hysterical laugh. 'Now I know why other people have one-night stands—so that they can maintain the illusion about the person they were with.' Her hand shaking, she dragged her phone out of her pocket. 'I'm leaving now and I don't want you to stop me. The children aren't watching so you don't have to be polite.'

Patrick's analytical mind was computing the data at his disposal. 'But if you're not pregnant—'

'If you say that word again, I might just punch

you.' She dialled a number, her fingers shaking. Then she lifted the phone to her ear.

'I just want to know why you came here.' Suddenly it was imperative to find that out. 'I want to understand why you came to see me.'

Her disparaging glance suggested that the answer was obvious. 'Because we had an amazing night, and the way you kiss might just possibly be the best thing that's ever happened to me and you seem to know more about my body than I do and although I actually did leave my knickers in your bedroom that night I— Hello, Jack?' She turned scarlet. 'No, no. It's me, Hayley— No, I didn't leave anything in the cab, that isn't what I meant— Well, I'm wearing them. I was talking to someone else— Well, no, not really.'

Resisting the impulse to smile, Patrick leaned forward and removed the phone from her hand. 'She just rang to wish you Merry Christmas, Jack,' he said smoothly, holding the phone to his ear. 'Thanks for delivering her safely. Great.' He held the phone out of reach as Hayley made a grab for it. 'Yes, and you, too.' He snapped the phone shut, his eyes on her face. 'Where were we? Oh, yes, you'd left your knickers in my bedroom and you were telling me that I'm an amazing kisser and that I seem to know more about your body than you do...'

'Don't get big-headed,' she warned darkly. 'I've realised that the reason you know more about my body than I do is because you've been *trained*—so it isn't a special skill. Actually, it's more like cheating.'

Still keeping the phone out of her reach, Patrick raised an eyebrow. 'It's cheating to know what turns you on?'

'Yes, because you sort of have an unfair advantage.' She eyed the phone in his hand. 'You spend your days with women.'

'Delivering their babies,' Patrick pointed out mildly, sliding the phone into his back pocket. 'And I can assure you that when I'm delivering babies, I'm not thinking about sex.'

'Well, you obviously know everything there is to know about...' Her face hot, she shifted in her chair. 'Oh, never mind. It's my fault for getting involved with an obstetrician. I can't believe we're actually having this conversation. I should never have come in, but I didn't want to upset your sweet, lovely son who, by the way, is far too nice to have a disreputable father like you.'

Smiling, Patrick reached down and hauled her to her feet, tightening his grip on her arms when she tried to wriggle away. After a few seconds he sucked in a breath. 'Actually, Hayley…' His voice was tight. 'You'd better not do that.'

'Do what?'

'Wriggle.'

'Well don't hold me, then.'

'I have to hold you,' he gritted, 'or you'll make it worse.'

'Make what worse?'

'My—er, problem.' His eyes dropped to her mouth and lingered. 'I have a rampant sex drive, remember? And you're… very attractive. And moving against certain parts of me…'

She froze like a child playing musical statues. 'Give me my phone back.'

'You can move your lips,' Patrick said dryly. 'That isn't the part of you that's causing me a problem.'

Her eyes threatened him. 'My phone.'

'No.' He gently removed the coat from her

shoulders and dropped it over the chair. Then he stroked her hair away from her face.

She tensed like a cat. '*What* do you think you're doing?'

He gave a slow smile. 'You said that kissing me was the best experience of your life.'

'That was before I knew the truth about you.' But her breathing quickened and he felt the chemistry flash between them.

'I didn't deceive you, Hayley. There was nothing dishonest about that night we spent together. I want to clear up that misunderstanding right now.'

Outside his kitchen the snow fell, dusting the window with soft white flakes.

Inside, the only sound was the slow jerk of her breathing and his own heartbeat as he struggled to control his shockingly powerful reaction.

Still not moving a muscle, her eyes were locked with his. 'You didn't tell me about your children. *How could you not mention your children?*'

'As I said, because that night was about you and me,' he said softly, sliding his fingers slowly through her hair. 'No one else.'

She closed her eyes and swayed slightly. 'Stop it. Stop touching me like that.'

'No.' His eyes slid to a shiny curl that had wrapped itself around his fingers. 'You're beautiful, Hayley.'

'You can't talk your way out of this, Patrick,' she whispered, and he lowered his head slowly.

'All right.' He murmured the words against her mouth, his body on fire. 'No talking. But that rule has to include you, too. And just to help you out…'

She gave a low moan and her lips parted against his. It was like being burned at the stake and Patrick's mind went blank.

And then she gave him a hard shove.

'No!' She backed away, her expression one of self-disgust, one hand raised, warning him to keep his distance. 'And you're *not* to do that again without warning me!'

Shaken by the erotic ache in his loins, Patrick hooked his thumbs into his front pockets to ease the pressure on his jeans. 'You want me to warn you when I'm intending to kiss you?'

'Yes. I need to prepare myself.'

Sensing that if he smiled he'd be in even greater trouble, he kept his expression deadpan. 'How much warning do you need? I mean, just so that I know. Are we talking seconds? Minutes?'

'Actually, forget it.' Visibly flustered, she pressed her fingers to her forehead. 'Just *don't* kiss me again, all right? Not unless you can learn to do it badly.'

'Could you define "badly"?' Patrick, who was feeling *extremely* bad, suspected he might have already qualified.

'Bad as in yucky.' Her glance was exasperated. 'The sort of kiss that makes you shudder and reach for a hairdryer. You know the sort!'

'I don't think I do.'

'Are you laughing at me again?'

'Absolutely not.'

'You *are* laughing at me!'

'All right, maybe,' he conceded, 'but in a good way.'

'There is no good way to mock someone.'

His amusement faded. 'I'm not mocking you. I'm complimenting you. You…surprise me. I've never met anyone quite like you before.'

'An embarrassing disaster, you mean? You don't need to point out that you're used to women who are far more sophisticated,' she mumbled, 'but you're not perfect either. Well, apart from the whole kissing thing, which you're actually pretty good at. And the…' She waved a hand. 'Well, you know. But there's plenty wrong with you. The worst of it being your very suspicious nature and your tendency towards the negative. I still can't believe you assumed I was pregnant. I mean, that has to be the most unromantic thing I've ever heard. What on *earth* would make you think that?'

'Hayley…' Trying to think cold thoughts to relieve the throbbing ache in his body, Patrick tried to focus on the conversation and not her mouth. 'It's Christmas Eve. I assumed that only the direst emergency would bring you to my doorstep in weather like this when everyone is decorating Christmas trees and preparing cranberry sauce.'

'I didn't know this was your doorstep.'

'But you came to Cumbria to find me.' He watched as the colour deepened in her cheeks. 'Unless I misunderstand what's going on here, you took this job because it would give you somewhere to stay over Christmas. And then you planned to track me down.'

'I've already told you, that was before I knew the real you.' Despite the bravado, he noticed that she was careful to keep a safe distance from him. *As if she didn't trust herself.*

'So you came all this way to find me.'

'Could you stop rubbing it in?'

'And now you're planning to leave.'

'Yes.'

'That isn't logical, Hayley.'

'Yes, well, logic doesn't have to be the basis for every decision.'

'Have you given any thought to where you're going to go?'

'No. Somewhere…' She gave a defensive shrug. 'Somewhere nice. With a big Christmas tree. And very possibly a log fire.'

'We have a big tree here. And a log fire.'

'Somewhere with a big tree and a log fire *where you don't live.*'

'Hayley, it's Christmas Eve,' he said gently. '"Somewhere"' generally needs to be booked a good six months in advance.'

'Then I'll take a train down to London or something.'

The thought of her sitting on a lonely, empty railway platform sent a chill down his spine. 'You answered the advert for a housekeeper—'

'That was before I knew this was your house.'

Feeling like a monster, Patrick sighed. 'I know I've made a bad impression but why don't we just start again, Hayley?'

'*Again?* Which part do you want to live through again?' Her expression was horrified. 'The part where I discover you have two children or the part where you assume that the only reason I've tracked you down is because I'm pregnant? Believe me, the whole thing was bad enough the first time. I'm not up for a repeat.'

Despite her flippant tone it was obvious that he'd offended her deeply and he was surprised to discover he felt ashamed. 'Hayley, in my defence, girls don't travel over six thousand miles to see a man they met just once unless—'

'Unless what? Unless they're pregnant and looking for a meal ticket? Was that what you were going to say? Just for the record, if I *had* been pregnant, I probably wouldn't even have told you.'

Patrick felt the sudden tension in his spine. 'You wouldn't?'

'I don't know.' Her voice rose. 'Maybe. Maybe not. Don't think I'm against marriage, because I'm not. But I think getting married just because you're having a baby is decidedly dodgy. Frankly I wish my mum *hadn't* married my stepdad. I often think we would have been happier just the two of us. The things is, you never really know, do you?' The information spilled from her like water from a fountain. 'I mean, if pregnancy was the reason for marriage, how would you ever know if that person loved you enough? You'd always wonder.'

As someone who had found himself in exactly that position, Patrick stared at her, unable to think of a suitable response.

'What's wrong now?' Her expression was exasperated. 'Did I say something wrong?'

'No. I'm just…surprised, again.' Patrick looked at her curiously, envying her ability to reveal intimate details of her life so unselfconsciously. 'You don't have any difficulty talking about private things, do you?'

'The reason most people don't talk about private things is because they're afraid of looking foolish or being judged, but I'm used to looking foolish *and* being judged.' She gave a little shrug that told him a great deal about her self-esteem. *Or lack of it.*

'Hayley—'

'You thought I was tracking you down because I needed money, didn't you?' She recoiled slightly. 'Why does everyone think that life has to be about money? Give me my phone.' Catching him off guard, she reached out and snatched the phone from his back pocket, her face scarlet as she stuffed it in her bag. 'I'll call a taxi from the road. A different taxi, *obviously,* given that Jack now knows everything there is to know about my sex life and even I don't feel comfortable getting in a cab with a stranger who knows that I once left my knickers in a man's bedroom. Go back to your children, Patrick, and have a good Christmas.' Sliding her bag onto her shoulder, she walked towards the door, but Patrick was before her, blocking the door, feeling as though he'd failed a test he hadn't even known he'd been taking.

She'd come all this way to see him again.

'Hayley.' His hand closed around her wrist and he felt the instant charge of electricity that had connected them from the first moment—*felt the pulse thrumming under her fingers.* 'Wait. You left your job in the States to track me down?'

People didn't do that, did they? *They didn't throw away a life they had for a life that they might have.*

She stilled, blinked several times and for a moment he thought she wasn't going to answer. 'Yes.' Her voice was thick. Clogged. 'That's what I did. It's called being impulsive. Or stupid. Can I ask you something?'

'Go on.'

'What would you have done if I hadn't left that morning?'

Patrick stared down at her, the tension throbbing between them. Then he gave a slow smile, watching with masculine satisfaction as the colour in her cheeks darkened. 'Yes,' he admitted. 'I would have done that.'

'I meant—would you have wanted to see me again?'

He sensed that it took her a lot of courage to ask the question. 'Yes. But it wasn't an option. I didn't want the job in Chicago and I wouldn't have asked you to come to Cumbria. As far as I could see, our relationship had no future.' He inhaled sharply. 'OK, I'm giving you a ten-second warning.'

'About what?'

'Five seconds.' His head lowered towards hers. 'Stay, Hayley. You answered an advert for a housekeeper. I need a housekeeper.'

And he wasn't going to let her leave.

'You didn't advertise for a housekeeper.'

'I would have done if I'd thought of it.' He pressed her up against the door, his mouth only a breath away from hers, 'I know you're angry with me. I know I've upset you. But that doesn't change what happened. There was nothing false about the night we spent together. Nothing.' He saw her breathing quicken, saw her gaze flicker briefly to his as the charge between them heated to dangerous levels. And then she looked away, as if it was the only way she could keep her sanity.

'As you keep telling me, it was a one-night stand.' Her eyes were fixed on one of Posy's childish drawings, haphazardly stuck to the kitchen wall. 'I should have left it at that.'

'I'm glad you didn't.'

She looked at him cautiously. 'I've never had a one-night stand before.'

'I know. I could tell.' Seeing her eyes widen, he gave a faint smile. 'That was why you ran off in the morning—you were embarrassed. And panicking. And thinking, *What have I done? I wish I'd woken up. I would have stopped you.*'

'Why didn't you mention your children, Patrick?' Even though they were alone in the room, she whispered the words. 'It isn't as if you didn't have the chance. We had dinner together. We *talked.*'

The chemistry between them was so intense he could taste it. 'Because for one night of my life I wasn't someone's father, or someone's doctor, or someone's boss,' Patrick said huskily. 'I was a man, enjoying the company of a beautiful woman. It was about you and me, Hayley. Nothing else. No one else. And now it's my turn. If I ask you something, will you answer me honestly?' He slid his hand behind her head, his eyes locked with hers.

'What?'

He gave a slow smile. 'Can you really cook a turkey?'

She stared up at him and then gave a reluctant laugh. 'That's what you want to ask me? Can I cook a turkey?'

'It's very important to me,' Patrick murmured,

his eyes dropping to her mouth. 'You have no idea how appalling untalented I am in the kitchen.'

'Don't worry about it. You're good in other rooms of the house.' Although her tone was mocking, the humour was back in her eyes.

'But that isn't going to help cook a turkey—unless we use a hairdryer. Stay, Hayley.'

She laughed but then gave a little shake of her head. 'I can't. We both know that would not be a good idea.' But he sensed her indecision and jumped on it with ruthless determination.

'If you'd ever tasted my Christmas dinner, you'd know it's an excellent idea.'

'I'm talking about the rest of it. I came here looking for the man I spent that night with but…' she took a breath '…you're not that man, Patrick. You have children. Responsibilities.'

Her opinion of him had clearly plummeted and he couldn't blame her for that. So far he'd made a mess of their meeting. 'I won't hurt my children, Hayley, that's true. They've been through enough because of me.'

'And that's a good enough reason for me not to stay, Patrick. It would be unfair on them. You obviously don't want them to know about us and I understand that.'

'This house has five large bedrooms, each with its own bathroom. You'd have space and privacy, somewhere warm and cosy to spend Christmas. A large tree and a log fire. Isn't that what you wanted?' It hadn't escaped him that she'd taken a job with a family. 'Alfie is so excited about you being here. He thinks Christmas lunch might be edible for once.'

'But—'

'Please, Hayley.' His voice was smooth and persuasive. 'I know I've made a mess of this and I know I've upset you. Yes, I was shocked to see you at first but…I really want you to stay. No strings. My son put an advert in the paper and you accepted the job. The job is yours. No more, no less. As for the rest of it, well…' He was standing so close to her that he could smell the floral fragrance of her shampoo mingling with the rose of her perfume. His senses communicated her scent to his libido and he was just deciding whether his previous warning counted when the door moved.

Reacting quickly, Patrick shifted Hayley out of

range and stepped back just as Alfie came charging into the kitchen, almost knocking into both of them.

'Dad, Posy's had an accident and the delivery van from the supermarket is at the door.'

CHAPTER THREE

HAYLEY held a packet of frozen peas against the little girl's leg, watching as Patrick soothed the child.

He was calm and concerned, his fingers gentle as he checked the joint. 'She's all right, Alfie— no permanent damage.'

Alfie was hovering anxiously. 'She banged herself *really* hard, Dad.'

'I'm sure she'll have a bruise, but nothing more.'

Hayley wondered whether she should borrow the frozen peas for her own bruises. Not the external ones—those would heal by themselves—but the internal ones. The ones caused by the realisation that their steamy night had been nothing more than sex for him.

It hadn't been a romantic encounter.

It hadn't been special, or earth-shattering.

It had simply been an opportunity for him to do what any red-blooded male would do in the same circumstances.

What had he said?

For one night I was a man, not a father.

But now he was a father again. And you didn't need a degree in psychology to see that his role as a parent was his first priority.

Hayley was trying really hard to hate him but it was impossible. How did you hate a man who clearly cared for his children so much? She found herself wondering exactly what had happened with his wife. If *she* were lucky enough to be married to a man like Patrick, she would have found a way to make the marriage work.

'How's that leg, Posy?' He stroked his daughter's hair gently and she buried her face in his chest.

'Uncle Daniel fix it.'

Patrick gave an amused smile. 'There isn't anything for him to fix. You'll be fine.' Catching Hayley's questioning look, he offered an explanation. 'My twin brother is a consultant in the accident and emergency department.'

'You have a twin? Identical?'

'We look similar but that's where the resemblance ends.'

'That's not true.' Alfie dived in. 'You both have big muscles. And you were both in the mountain rescue team.'

Patrick shifted Posy slightly. 'That's right. We were.'

'You could still do it.' Alfie picked up Posy's velvet comforter and sneaked it into his sister's hand. 'We wouldn't mind, would we, Pose? We'd be OK here. I'm almost old enough to look after you.'

Posy grinned at her brother but showed no sign of relinquishing her grip on her dad. There was something about the sight of the young child clinging to her father that brought a lump to Hayley's throat.

Oh, great.

She was going to embarrass herself yet again.

And just because the guy was patient and kind to his daughter. Really, she needed to get out more.

So he was good with kids—*so what?*

Plenty of men were good with kids.

It was just that Patrick managed to do it in a way that didn't diminish his masculinity. His hands were firm. Sure. He had a quiet confidence that soothed the child as much as his calm voice.

'I can imagine you in the mountain rescue team,' Hayley muttered, and then wished she hadn't when he lifted an eyebrow in question. 'I mean, you just look the outdoor type,' she said lamely. 'What exactly do you do? You go out into the mountains and find people?' *And slide down ropes, and save lives and generally behave like a hero.*

Nothing particularly attractive about that, she told herself firmly. He was just doing a job.

'People often find themselves in trouble in the fells.'

'Fells?'

'In the Lake District we call the mountains fells.' He checked Posy's knee again. 'People often underestimate the peaks here. They go out wearing the wrong footgear and with the wrong equipment. And that makes plenty of work for the mountain rescue team. I did it for a few years—my brother still does it. He doesn't have kids so he can take off at short notice and come back eight hours later without having to worry.'

'Do you miss it?'

His eyes narrowed, as if he hadn't asked himself that question. 'No.' His gaze slid to Alfie and Hayley sensed that he was protecting his son's feelings.

Being a single dad had obviously demanded some big sacrifices.

He'd given up something he loved so that he could spend more time with his children.

Her cheeks pink, Hayley looked away from him, telling herself that he wasn't *that* attractive. All right, so he could kiss, but just because he had a particular skill in that area, it didn't make him a good person.

There was certainly no reason for her stomach to feel as though it had been left on the fast spin cycle of the washing machine.

'Dad, is there any chocolate in those shopping bags?' Alfie was looking hopefully at the supermarket bags that had been heaped by the door ready to be unpacked. 'Did you order something to go on the Christmas tree?'

'Let's go and take a look.' Patrick tried to ease the little girl off his lap but she clung to him, her thumb in her mouth, her fist locked in his thick jumper. 'Sweetheart, Daddy has to spend some time in the kitchen or Christmas isn't going to happen.' He bent his head and kissed his daughter's blonde head, the contrast between strong and vulnerable so vivid that Hayley sighed. Just the sight of Posy's sweet red stockings against the hard muscle of his thighs was enough to make her tummy tumble.

Oh, help, she didn't want to feel this way.

This man was no saint.

He'd had sex with her. He hadn't told her he had children.

'I'll sort out the shopping.' Desperate to look at something other than his unshaven jaw and the tempting line of his lips, Hayley scrambled to her feet, the peas still in her hand. 'Have you finished with these?'

His gaze searching, Patrick nodded. 'Yes. Her leg is fine. But I don't expect you to unload the shopping, Hayley.'

'It's fine. Really.' Decisions, decisions. She really *hated* making decisions and she was going to have to make one now. Stay or go. Stay or go. Go, *obviously*. After what had happened, it would be just too embarrassing to stay here, wouldn't it?

On the other hand, where was she going to go, this late on Christmas Eve?

It would be more sensible to stay. More practical. The last thing she needed was to find herself with nowhere to go. Yes, she'd stay. But *not* because of Patrick. Her decision had nothing to do with the fact that this man knew how to turn a woman from a solid to a liquid.

She gave a careless shrug, hoping that she looked suitably casual. 'You haven't given me a job description, but I presume that unloading shopping is the responsibility of the housekeeper.'

Alfie gave a squeal of delight. 'You're staying? Yay! We'll have a proper Christmas lunch.' He leapt over to the bags and hugged Hayley, and she hugged him back, a lump in her throat. Over the top of his head, she met Patrick's steady gaze.

'You're staying?'

'Yes.' She gave an awkward shrug. 'And let's just hope it doesn't prove to be the second biggest mistake of my life.'

'The first one being?'

Hayley gave him a meaningful look and guided Alfie towards the bags. 'Come and show me where everything goes, Alfie.' She needed to keep busy to stop her brain from working overtime. So far it hadn't done a good job. Her over-active mind had taken her down routes that had brought her nothing but embarrassment.

Next time she saw a happy ending on the horizon she was going to reprogramme her internal sat nav.

'There's chocolate in those bags.' Alfie bounded over the bags with all the energy of an over-excited puppy. 'When do we put the turkey in the oven?'

'Not until the morning.' Hayley smiled at him. 'Actually, I think you can cook it overnight in the Aga, but we're not going to do that. We'll cook it tomorrow.'

As she unloaded bags and found her way around Patrick's state-of-the-art kitchen, Hayley couldn't help wondering if she'd done the wrong thing by staying.

Patrick knew exactly how she felt about him— how could he not? She'd crossed an ocean to find him. Cringing with embarrassment, she put a net of sprouts on the table ready to be prepared. Patrick, on the other hand, had given away nothing.

Frowning slightly, Hayley tipped a container of

fresh cranberries into a pan and reached for an orange.

What had he told her about himself?

Precisely nothing.

The only information she had about him was the obvious stuff—like his two children.

He had told her he was divorced, but he hadn't told her anything else, had he?

She added the zest and juice of an orange to the simmering cranberries.

He hadn't told her why his relationship had fallen apart. He hadn't told her why his wife wasn't spending Christmas with them.

Leaving the cranberries to simmer, she dug around in the fridge, searching for the ingredients for stuffing, her heart rate doubling as Patrick walked into the kitchen, Posy in his arms. 'Do you have any pork?'

Patrick looked at her blankly and sat Posy on the nearest chair. 'Pork? As in a joint of pork? I thought we were having turkey.'

'I need pork for the stuffing,' Hayley said patiently, and Patrick gave a lopsided smile.

'I'm lucky if I can get the thing in the oven, let alone stuff it.'

'It just helps the flavour. Don't worry,' Hayley muttered, 'I'll see what you have in your fridge.' She returned to the fridge, found some sausages and parsley and helped herself to an egg. 'This will do. I don't suppose you have any chestnuts?'

'I think there's a box in the larder, but they're probably past their sell-by date.' He produced them and Hayley checked the date and emptied them onto her chopping board.

'They're fine. Alfie, can you pass me an apple from the bowl?'

'I don't like apples.' He wrinkled his nose in disgust and she smiled.

'It's going in our stuffing. You won't taste it.' As she chopped, stirred and cooked, Alfie buzzed around her, helping.

'What's that you're doing now?'

'Bread sauce.' She infused the milk with an onion and cloves. 'It's delicious. If I do it now, it will be one less thing to worry about tomorrow.'

Alfie was watching, wide-eyed with admiration. 'Who taught you how to do all this stuff?'

'I taught myself. I had to. No one else in my family can cook.' She took the milk off the heat.

'Well, they probably could cook if they tried. Everyone can cook if they try.'

'My dad can't.' Alfie stood on a chair, slowly stirring cranberry sauce, his lower lip locked between his teeth. 'And he *has* tried. His cooking is a disaster.'

'Thanks Alfie,' Patrick said dryly, and Alfie shrugged.

'Even your pasta is gluey.'

'You're not cooking it in enough water,' Hayley said absently. 'You need a large pan so that it doesn't stick together. That looks done, Alfie. Take the saucepan off the heat and put it on the mat to cool. Good boy.'

'This is so brilliant. Like being in a restaurant or something.' Alfie lifted the pan carefully and put it on the table. 'Now what?'

'We let it cool and then we put it in the fridge.'

Alfie watched, wide-eyed, as she deftly made little stuffing balls. 'Wow. You are so clever at that. If you're here with us, who is cooking Christmas dinner for your family?'

Hopefully someone really inept.

Hayley gave a weak smile. 'They'll probably go to a hotel to eat.'

'I bet they miss you.'

Feeling Patrick's gaze on her face, Hayley tried not to reveal her thoughts. *He saw too much.*

'Yes, I'm sure they miss me.' Like lions missing an antelope. No one to pick on.

Patrick leaned forward and pulled the pan further onto the mat, avoiding disaster. 'You have brothers and sisters?'

'Two stepbrothers. One stepsister.' She kept her tone neutral but knew he wasn't fooled.

'You lived with a stepfamily?'

Oh, God, he wasn't going to let it go, was he? 'My dad left when I was little. My mum married her boss. He already had three children. End of story.' Except it wasn't the end of the story and she had a feeling he knew it.

'My mum left, too.' Alfie said the words casually but Hayley sensed the depth of emotion behind his simple confession and felt as though her heart was being tugged out of her chest.

Out of the corner of her eye she saw Patrick still, but Alfie was looking at her and she knew he was waiting for her to respond.

Suddenly she wished she'd done a degree in child psychology—at least then she would have known just the right thing to say. 'That must have been very difficult for you.'

'It was sort of difficult.' Alfie gave an awkward shrug. 'She went on Christmas Eve. Two years ago.'

'Christmas Eve?' Horrified, Hayley's eyes flew to Patrick but he was watching his son.

'We're doing pretty well, aren't we, Alfie?'

'Brilliantly. We're a team. Team Buchannan, that's us. High five, Dad.' Slapping his palm against his father's, Alfie slid off the chair and walked over to the fridge. 'The only thing wrong is that no one in our team is good at cooking. Sometimes Stella helps us, and that's good. She can make gingerbread men. Can you make gingerbread men, Hayley?'

Still choked at the thought that their mother had left on Christmas Eve, Hayley struggled to answer. 'Yes,' she said huskily, feeling a rush of anger towards a woman she didn't even know. 'I can make gingerbread men. Who is Stella?'

Patrick stirred. 'A friend.'

Friend? Hayley felt a stab of jealousy and then realised how ridiculous it was to feel jealous of this man. They didn't have a relationship, did they?

'Stella used to be engaged to Uncle Daniel but he didn't want to get married because he thinks he won't be a good father.' Alfie pushed the fridge door shut, a yoghurt in his hand. 'Which is rubbish, because he's pretty cool at a lot of things, but he doesn't think so, so he told Stella that he wouldn't marry her. That was the same Christmas Mum left, so Stella came here and cooked lunch and it was brilliant. And she and Dad drank a lot.' He dug a spoon out of the drawer and Hayley's eyes flew to Patrick, who rolled his eyes in apology, his neutral expression revealing nothing about what must have been a hideous time.

Oblivious to his father's discomfort, Alfie dug the spoon into the yoghurt. 'And then Stella went away for ages because she was so upset that Daniel wouldn't marry her, but she still sent me nice presents. Then she came back.' He licked the spoon. 'And then she and Uncle Daniel were trying not to kiss each other all the time, and—'

'Alfie.' Patrick's tone was mild. 'Enough. Eat your yoghurt and stop talking.'

'I'm just telling Hayley about our family.'

'You've told her enough.'

'But I haven't finished.' The spoon still poised in the air, Alfie frowned at his father. 'I haven't told her the best bit.'

'Go on, then,' Patrick said wearily, rubbing his fingertips across his forehead. 'Tell her the best bit. Whatever that is. But make it quick.'

'Uncle Daniel is going to propose to Stella. Tomorrow.'

Patrick made a choked sound and suddenly sat upright. 'He is *what?*'

'He is going to propose to her.' Smug now he had his father's attention, Alfie slowly finished his yoghurt. 'He told me. I saw the ring. He's putting it in her Secret Santa—you know, you buy a present for someone at work, and—'

'I know what Secret Santa is.' Patrick interrupted him impatiently. 'What's this about a ring? Since when has my brother decided to propose and how come you know about it?'

'I helped him decide. He wanted to marry her, really, but Stella wants lots of babies and Uncle Daniel is worried he won't be a good dad. So I sort of helped him out with some tips.' He saw his father's astonished look and shrugged. 'It wasn't that hard. Uncle Daniel was OK when he looked after us when you were in America. Posy and I liked being with him. I just told him that. And he listened.'

Hayley couldn't hold back her laughter. 'So your brother is getting married?'

'So it would seem.' Patrick ran a hand over the back of his neck and looked at his son as though he were a stranger. 'Where do you get all this information?'

'Uncle Daniel and I had a long talk this morning. And, anyway, I see things.' Alfie dropped the empty yoghurt pot in the bin. 'I know about se— I mean, *you know what*. I can't say the "s" word in front of Posy because she's too young.'

'Quite right,' Patrick said faintly, 'and so are you, frankly.'

'Dad, you're behind the times. Two of the boys in my class have girlfriends.'

Patrick closed his eyes. 'Alfie, you are ten years old. You are *not* having a girlfriend.'

'It's all right,' Alfie said kindly, 'you can stop panicking. All the girls in my class are pretty yucky, to be honest. I wouldn't want to kiss any of them. At the moment I prefer football.'

'I suppose I should be thankful for small

mercies,' Patrick muttered under his breath, casting Hayley a look of comical disbelief. 'How did we get onto this subject? I thought we were talking about *your* family?'

'My family is boring by comparison.' She laughed and Alfie looked at her closely.

'But they're the reason you moved to America? Because they made you feel like you couldn't do anything? If you ask me, they're dumb. And anyone who can cook like you shouldn't have to prove anything to anyone.' Having made that announcement, he strolled out of the room, leaving Hayley staring after him.

Patrick cleared his throat. 'I apologise for Alfie. He's always been pretty direct. Probably my fault.'

'I think he's very special.' Hayley rescued the bread sauce, desperately wishing that Alfie hadn't left the room. Without him she was too aware of Patrick.

Oh, God, she shouldn't be here.

She'd taken a risk—*exposed her feelings*—and now she felt like an utter fool because she had nowhere to hide.

He *knew* how she felt about him.

And she knew how he felt about her.

She stirred the bread sauce vigorously to avoid having to look at him.

He'd taken advantage of being away from his children to have some easy sex. And she'd been easy sex. And she was angry and humiliated that she'd allowed her dreamy personality to turn a steamy encounter into something more.

Even though she was trying to be pragmatic about the whole thing, his assumption that her reason for tracking him down must be because she was pregnant had crushed her. His reaction was so far removed from the one she'd expected. She'd honestly thought he'd felt the same way about her as she did about him. Of *course* she had or she would never have travelled all this way and risked making a fool of herself. It hadn't occurred to her that she *was* making a fool of herself.

Alfie bounced back into the room. 'Come and see your room, Hayley. You'll love it. It has a sloping ceiling and a *really* cool bathroom with a drench thing.'

Hayley looked down at him for a long moment and then turned her head to look at Patrick.

He held her gaze and something flickered between them.

Hayley dismissed it as her imagination. She wasn't making that mistake again. *Wasn't assuming there was a connection where there was none.*

'I'd like you to show me my room,' she said to Alfie, and he grinned happily.

'Your room is right next to mine. If you're lonely, you can sleep in my spare bunk.'

Hayley couldn't help smiling. 'That's really generous of you, Alfie. I might just do that.' He was the sweetest, most engaging child she'd ever met. 'Come on, then. Show me the room.'

Relieved to escape from Patrick's brooding gaze for a short time, Hayley followed Alfie up the beautiful wooden staircase and up to the top floor of the barn. He pushed open a door and Hayley gave a gasp of surprise because nothing had prepared her for the breathtakingly beautiful view from the room.

Floor-to-ceiling windows faced open fields, framing the snow-covered trees and the mountains behind. 'Oh, my goodness,' she said weakly, 'It's stunning.' *Was he a millionaire or something?* The house was *incredible.*

'You should see my dad's bedroom. It's *huge.*

So is his bed. Mind you, he needs an enormous bed because Posy often crawls in with him in the middle of the night.' Alfie darted across the bedroom and pushed open another door. 'This is your bathroom. The window goes all the way along so you can still see the view from the bath. You've gone really red—I suppose you're worrying about someone seeing you naked, but they won't. We don't have any neighbours, which is quite useful when Posy is having one of her tantrums.'

Hayley, whose colour had more to do with inappropriate thoughts involving Patrick's bed than modesty, managed a smile. 'Thanks. I'll remember that.'

'I'm just saying that you don't need to worry too much about wandering around with no clothes on.'

'There is absolutely no way I'll be wandering around with no clothes on,' Hayley assured him hastily, shrinking at the thought of bumping into Patrick in anything less than full clothing.

She'd already left one pair of knickers on his bedroom floor. That was more than enough.

From now on she would be making no moves

at all, except ones that took her in the opposite direction.

'I thought Dad would be really mad with me for advertising for a housekeeper,' Alfie confided, 'but I think he's pleased now that you're going to be cooking the turkey. He's *hopeless* at it.'

'Well, if we want a delicious lunch without a nervous breakdown, we'd better go and finish our preparations.' Hayley held out her hand. 'Are you ready, Chef?'

Alfie grinned. 'Ready.'

Another layer of snow fell overnight and Hayley woke to a world so impossibly beautiful that for a moment she didn't move. Warm and snug under the soft duvet, she lay there, listening to church bells chiming in the distance.

Christmas morning.

And for once she didn't have to brace herself to face her family. *To try and be someone she wasn't.*

There was a tap on the door and Patrick walked in, a mug in his hand. He was wearing a pair of black jeans and his jaw was dark with stubble. 'You wanted to be woken at eight…'

Oh, my, he looked good in the morning—heavy lidded and unshaven…

'Yes. I want to get the turkey in the oven so that we can eat at a decent time.' Hayley decided it was safer to look at the mug he was holding, rather than him. 'Thanks for the tea.'

'I thought it might help you wake up. I'm guessing you're jet-lagged. What time did you get to sleep?'

'Oh—not sure,' Hayley mumbled, pulling the duvet up to her chin. 'Late. Still feels like the middle of the night.' She wasn't going to confess that her appallingly disturbed night had had everything to do with him and nothing to do with the time difference. 'Thanks for the tea.'

'The children are going to wait until you're down before they open their presents.'

'They don't have to do that.' Hayley was dying to drink the tea but she didn't want to expose any part of her body while he was in the room. It was bad enough being in bed while he was standing there. It felt intimate. And she was doing her best to avoid all suggestion of intimacy. 'But I'm not family or anything. I was going to spend the morning in the kitchen. Let you get on with it.'

'You're living with us, Hayley,' he said mildly. 'You're one of the family.'

In her dreams.

She was so aware of him that she was relieved to have the kitchen as an excuse to hide.

In the end she did join them for present opening, watching wistfully as the children tore paper off parcels and squealed with delight.

'I have a present for Hayley.' Alfie vanished and then reappeared, carrying two kittens.

'Oh!' Hayley gasped in delight and Patrick groaned.

'Alfie, you can't—'

'My cat had four kittens…' Alfie placed the kittens in Hayley's lap '…and Dad says I can only keep two. So I'm giving you the other two. I want them to go to someone nice.'

The kittens snuggled into each other and Hayley stared down at them with a lump in her throat. 'They're gorgeous.'

'Alfie…' Patrick ran his hand over his jaw '…you can't just give someone an animal. Hayley doesn't have anywhere to keep them.'

'Well, they're hers just for Christmas, then,' Alfie said stubbornly. 'While she's staying here. I'll let her feed them and things.'

'I think she's going to be busy enough feeding us,' Patrick muttered, but Hayley shook her head, enchanted by the kittens.

'They're beautiful, Alfie. And wherever I go after Christmas, I'll make sure it's somewhere I can have kittens. Thank you.'

Later, while Alfie and Posy were playing with their presents and her kittens were curled up on the sofa asleep, Hayley slipped away to the kitchen.

This was the perfect Christmas, wasn't it?

Snow falling outside the window and children laughing in the next room.

She worked steadily and without fuss and when she eventually placed the bronzed turkey in the centre of the table, Alfie gasped and clapped his hands.

'For once it looks the way it always looks in the pictures. Thanks, Hayley. I'm starving.'

Lunch was a noisy, happy affair. Crackers were pulled, jokes were read and paper hats were worn, although Hayley had to make use of a roll of tape in order to stop Posy's from falling down around her neck.

She was just setting light to the Christmas pudding when Patrick's mobile rang.

He fished it out of his pocket, frowning as he saw the number. 'Excuse me—I need to answer this. Tom?' Moving away from the table, he strolled to the other end of the living room and Hayley's gaze lingered on his broad shoulders.

'Hayley, the pudding is going to fall off the plate,' Alfie said helpfully, and she gave a start and concentrated on what she was doing.

'Pudding?' But she could still hear Patrick talking.

'Well, it's her first labour… No, I wouldn't think so… Calm down, will you?'

'Someone is in trouble,' Alfie predicted, pouring brandy sauce onto his pudding. 'Is this alcoholic? Am I going to get drunk?'

'You're not going to get drunk.'

'Good, because the next thing that's going to happen is that Dad is going to come off the phone and say he has to go to the hospital.'

Patrick slipped the phone back into his pocket

and strode back to them. 'I'm really sorry but I'm going to have to go to the hospital.'

'Told you.' Alfie leaned across the table and pushed the candle away from his sister's fingers. 'Don't touch that, Pose, or you'll be going to the hospital too. In an ambulance. What is it this time, Dad? Twins?'

'No.' Patrick looked distracted. 'Tom Hunter's wife has gone into labour. And he's worried about her.'

'Tom works with Dad,' Alfie told Hayley, and Patrick gave a frown of apology.

'Sorry, Hayley.'

'It's fine. Do you want pudding or are you going straight in? I can stay with the children.'

'It's more complicated than that.' Patrick ran a hand over the back of his neck, and then looked at her thoughtfully. 'You're a midwife.'

Hayley slowly put the pudding down on the table, wondering where this was leading. 'You know I'm a midwife.'

'We're chronically short of midwives at the moment—particularly over the Christmas period. People are being struck down by flu and apparently there isn't an agency midwife to be had north of Birmingham. Tom's worried that Sally won't have continuity of care.'

'I registered with the agency when I arrived in the UK, but I haven't—'

'You're already registered?' Patrick's face cleared. 'Fantastic. In that case, is there any way I can persuade you to come to the hospital with me?'

'No way!' Alfie shot to his feet, his eyes fierce. 'You are *not* leaving us with Mrs Thornton on Christmas Day! I want to stay with Hayley.'

'You can both come to the hospital,' Patrick said immediately, scooping Posy out of her chair. 'Alfie, go and pack a backpack with all her toys and a change of clothes. You can play in my office. Bring some DVDs.'

'Yippee!' Alfie bounced towards the Christmas tree where the presents were still scattered. 'There's always loads of chocolate at the hospital. Will Aunty Mags be there?'

'Yes.'

'W-wait a minute,' Hayley stammered. 'I can't just turn up and work. I'm not sure they'd want me to just—'

'I'll call Human Resources on the way in and they can do whatever it is they need to do.'

'Human Resources?' Hayley gaped at him. 'But it's Christmas Day! They're not working.'

'My dad is really important,' Alfie said proudly as he reappeared, carrying a bulging rucksack. 'If he says someone has to do something, they have to do it.'

Patrick lifted an eyebrow. 'I hadn't noticed that rule applying to you.'

Alfie grinned. 'That's different. I'm your son. I get special treatment.' He grabbed Posy and manoeuvred her into her coat. 'Come on, Pose. We're going to have fun.'

CHAPTER FOUR

'SHE'S dilated less than two centimetres in the last four hours but she doesn't want me to intervene,' Tom said in a raw tone, his face pale and tired. 'And I feel helpless. I'm an obstetrician! I've delivered hundreds of women, but I can't think straight.'

'That's because she's your wife.' Patrick switched on the television in his office, pulled up two chairs and settled the children. 'It's different when you're emotionally involved.'

'Well, you know what Sally's like—stubborn. I think the time has come to intervene but she refuses to even consider anything that constitutes aggressive management.'

'I'll take a look at her.' Patrick removed his jacket and slung it over the chair. 'This is Hayley. She's going to be Sally's personal midwife.'

Suddenly the focus of attention, Hayley turned pink. She wanted to open her mouth and protest that he'd never even seen her work, but Patrick was already ushering her along the corridor.

Without pausing, he pushed open the first door he came to and walked into the delivery suite.

Hayley looked around her in surprise. The room was light, bright and homely, with views across the mountains from the large picture window.

A petite woman sat on the bed in the middle of the room, concentrating on her breathing.

'Sal?' His voice gentle, Patrick strode across to the bed, leaned forward and kissed her on both cheeks. 'You really pick your moments. I haven't eaten my Christmas pudding.'

'You're a lousy obstetrician, Ric,' the woman moaned. 'You told me there was no way this baby would come until Boxing Day.'

'I hate to disillusion you, babe, but it could well be Boxing Day.' Patrick looked at the clock and then at the chart by the bed. 'Not exactly motoring, are you?'

'It's definitely time to intervene,' Tom said gruffly. 'Sally, I really think you should—'

'If you don't shut up, Tom Hunter, I'm never

speaking to you again. And I'm certainly not sleeping with you again. Not if this is the outcome.' Sally screwed up her face as another pain hit her and Hayley saw Tom tense helplessly.

'Sally—'

Like a wounded tigress, Sally growled at him. 'Patrick, talk some sense into him. And here's a hint—while you're having that conversation I don't want to hear the words *amniotomy*, *oxytocin infusion*, *ventouse* or *forceps*. And I *definitely* don't want to hear *Caesarean section*. Or I am never again cooking you my special crispy duck or my lemon tart. Got that?'

Patrick grinned. 'I think we'll have this conversation outside. That way, at least I'll protect my future dining prospects.' He took Tom's arm and guided him out of the room, leaving Hayley alone with the woman.

Her eyes bright with pain, Sally glanced at her. 'Sorry—I love Tom. Honestly I do, but he's in a state and he's making me worse. We haven't been introduced—' She caught her breath as another pain hit and Hayley hurried across to her, sensing that the other woman was feeling isolated and alone.

'You're not breathing properly,' Hayley murmured, sliding her arm round Sally's narrow shoulders. 'You're talking too much—thinking about everyone else and not yourself.'

'That's because my husband is having a meltdown,' Sally gritted, and Hayley rubbed her back gently.

'Patrick will sort him out. You think about yourself. You're obviously struggling with the pain. Do you want some gas and air?'

'Nothing at the moment.' Sally shifted on the bed. 'God, it hurts. Isn't it typical? I can't believe I'm still only four centimetres. I should have delivered by now. That's what happens when your husband is an obstetrician. You're doomed. Fate intervenes to give you the worst delivery possible.'

'Don't think like that. We just need to have a plan and try and help you relax.' Relieved that she'd had the foresight to grab her bag before she'd left Patrick's barn, Hayley reached inside and pulled out a small bottle. 'See if you like the smell of this.'

She unscrewed the cap and held it under Sally's nose.

'Nice.'

'It is, isn't it? It's an aromatherapy oil I used a lot in America. Perfectly safe in pregnancy and labour. Would you like me to massage your shoulders? I find that sometimes it helps and you really need to relax.'

'At this point I'm willing to try anything,' Sally gasped. 'It really does smell good. Takes your mind off hospitals.'

'Close your eyes and just think about your breathing,' Hayley soothed, lifting Sally's T-shirt just enough to allow her to massage the woman's back.

Sally closed her eyes and breathed out. 'All right—that's better. Actually, it feels unbelievably good. But I think my husband needs it more than me.'

'We're not thinking about your husband right now,' Hayley reminded her, 'we're thinking about you.'

'Oh, yes, I remember.' Sally was silent for a few minutes, only the slight change in her breathing indicating a change in her pain levels. 'You are very clever. Where did Patrick find you? I'm starting to feel a bit better. Just don't let my panicking husband back in here. I've never seen him like this. He's Mr Cool. Every bit as calm as Patrick. And suddenly he's lost it and turned into the worst kind of panicking man.'

'It's because he loves you.' Hayley's hands moved gently, smoothing and soothing. 'Have you thought about using the pool, Sally? I assume they have one here.'

Sally sighed. 'Tom isn't keen. *Don't* ask me why.'

'It's just that I think you might find it relaxing. In my experience women tend to need less pain relief and they just find the whole experience more satisfying. I think it might be perfect for you.'

'Well, I certainly like all your other ideas. I think I might just want to be massaged by you all the way through my labour,' Sally murmured. 'You are so good at that. Another contraction coming…'

'So focus on your breathing.' Hayley coached her quietly and then glanced up to see Patrick and Tom standing by the door. She wondered how long they'd been there. Watching.

'Tom, Hayley thinks I should use the birthing pool and I agree with her.' Sally spoke firmly, as if she was expecting argument. 'I want to give it a try.'

Tom glared at Hayley and then let out a breath

and looked at Patrick. 'I don't think it's a good idea. What do you think?'

'I think it's up to Sally. There's no medical reason why she shouldn't.' Calm and relaxed, Patrick walked over to the bed. 'What I'd like to do is examine you properly, check on the baby and then we can make a decision together.'

'I don't need an obstetrician—I need a midwife.'

Tom sighed. 'Please, Sal…'

'Oh, for goodness' sake.' Sally flopped back against the pillows. 'Tom, go and get a cup of coffee.'

'But—'

'If you really want Patrick to examine me, fine, but I don't want you here while he does it. Hayley can chaperone, although I'm sure Patrick isn't exactly having indecent thoughts about me at this point. I'm about as sexy as a whale.'

Patrick laughed and moved over to the sink to wash his hands. 'I'm saying nothing. This is one of those conversations where a man can only ever be wrong. Tom, do me a favour and check on my kids, will you? They're in my office. Maggie was going to get them some chocolate and drinks but I don't want them being sick on the carpet.'

With obvious reluctance Tom left the room and Sally sighed.

'He's worried.'

'Understandably.' Patrick listened to the foetal heart rate. 'But his anxiety is stressing you and you already have enough stress. When I've checked on you, I'm going to go and calm him down.'

'How are you going to do that? Knock him unconscious? What do you think about Hayley's water-birth idea?'

Patrick looked at Hayley, his gaze quizzical. 'Persuade me.'

Was he testing her? 'Stress can lead to reduced uterine activity and dystocia.' Confident in her own skills, Hayley explained her reasoning. 'Which is why I think you should consider water. It can help relaxation and pain relief. I think it's worth a try. If she makes no progress, you can always think again.'

Patrick finished his examination and straightened. 'You're four centimetres, Sally.'

'Is that all?' Sally gave a groan and closed her eyes. 'Tom is going to have a breakdown. And I might have one with him.'

'Why are you lying on the bed?' Hayley sat

down next to her, her voice soft. 'I wonder whether you should mobilise for an hour or so. Walk around the department with me—see if we can get you moving a bit faster. Then go for the pool.'

Sally gave her an ironic look. 'You want me to run a marathon?'

Hayley grinned. 'No. I had in mind more of a stroll down the corridor, talking about shoes and similarly frivolous distractions.'

Sally stared at her. 'How do you know I like shoes?'

'Because I've been admiring your shoes since I walked into the room.' Hayley's gaze slid to the pair of silver mules that Sally had tucked under the chair. 'I love them.'

Patrick backed away, shaking his head. 'I'm not qualified to participate in a discussion about shoes. I'll go and handle Tom.' He glanced at Hayley, a smile playing around his mouth. 'I like your plan. You've managed women labouring in water?'

'Yes. All the time.' She had no doubts about her abilities as a midwife but she realised that he knew nothing about that side of her. He hadn't worked with her, had he? Their only professional contact had been when she'd shown him around the department and that hadn't included any clinical work. 'Who do I speak to about the pool?'

'I'll get someone onto it now. You need to change—Maggie has found you a set of scrubs that should fit. You can use my office.' Patrick took a pen out of his pocket and wrote in the notes. 'Get walking, Sally. When it gets too much, try the pool. Hayley can examine you again in four hours.'

Sally grabbed his hand. 'Tom is *seriously* worried.'

'I know that,' Patrick said gently. 'But we're watching you. The baby is happy at the moment. You're the one who isn't happy and we're going to do something about that.'

He was so good with the patients, Hayley thought wistfully as she helped Sally put on her shoes.

'Let's go for that walk. I can change in a minute.' Hayley slid her arm through Sally's and walked with her to the door. 'I don't suppose jeans matter for walking up and down the corridor. I can't imagine anyone in authority is going to be in today.'

'Patrick's the highest authority here anyway.'

Sally gritted her teeth and rubbed her abdomen while Hayley looked at her in surprise.

'Really?'

'He runs the unit, didn't you know? He's astonishing—so bright. And really nice with it. He's the only person Tom is likely to listen to.'

Hayley wondered whether Sally knew the details of Patrick's divorce.

She didn't like to ask, but Sally's mind was obviously moving in the same direction because she paused in the corridor and looked at Hayley curiously. 'So how do you know Patrick?'

'Oh.' Hayley made a conscious effort not to spill everything out. 'I applied for a job as his housekeeper over Christmas.'

'He advertised for a housekeeper?'

'Not exactly.' Drawn to Sally's warmth and unable to help herself, Hayley told Sally the story of the advert. She laughed.

'That's brilliant. Good for Alfie. Oops— another contraction coming.' She leaned on Hayley, breathing steadily. After a few moments she straightened. 'Actually, I quite like being upright. Hi, Maggie.' She smiled at a midwife who approached them.

'How are you doing, Sally? And you must be our Christmas miracle.' Smiling warmly, she pushed a set of clean scrubs into Hayley's hands. 'Alfie has told me all about your amazing cooking skills. I'm sorry to interrupt your Christmas Day but I can't tell you how relieved I am to have you helping us out today.'

'I—I'm pleased to help,' Hayley stammered, touched by how generous these strangers were. They didn't even know her, for goodness' sake. 'I *am* a qualified midwife.'

Maggie gave a delighted laugh. 'I'm hoping so—we're trusting you with our consultant's wife so you're going to need more than the ability to baste a turkey.'

The consultant's wife.

Hayley gave Sally a weak smile. 'No pressure, then.'

'You've met my husband,' Sally said dryly. 'There'll be nothing but pressure. If Patrick doesn't keep him busy he'll be hanging over you, watching everything you're doing.'

'That doesn't bother me.' Hayley rubbed Sally's back gently. 'I've been working in America—

everyone watches everything there. It's the land of litigation.'

Maggie looked curious. 'Ah, yes—Alfie mentioned that you've been working in America. What a coincidence—our Patrick was in America just a few weeks ago, interviewing for a job.'

'Really?' Hayley squeaked the word, searching for ways of extracting herself from what was fast developing into a conversation she didn't want to have.

'Oh—that hurts.' With a gasp, Sally clutched her. 'Could we go back to the room, Hayley?'

'Of course.' Concerned, Hayley slipped her arm round her new friend, sending Maggie a look of apology. 'Thanks for the scrubs. I'll change in a minute.'

'No hurry. We owe you.' Maggie watched them walk slowly down the corridor. 'And the birthing pool will be ready whenever you are.'

Hayley pushed open the door to Sally's room and helped her inside.

The other woman immediately straightened and gave her a look. 'All right, I rescued you from the inquisition—my price is that you tell me the truth.'

Hayley stared at her. 'You weren't having a contraction?'

'No, but I will be in another minute so could you get to the juicy part fairly quickly?' Sally lumbered over to the bed. 'And the more detail the better, please. Good sex is a thing of the past for me. Whoever said that women always feel sexy in pregnancy had never put on this much weight. I can't imagine why Tom would want to touch me, looking like this.'

'You look gorgeous, Sally.'

'No, it's my shoes that look gorgeous.' Sally eased herself onto the edge of the bed. 'I just look fat. Oh…' She screwed up her face and started to breath steadily, trying to work through the contraction.

Hayley put her hand on Sally's abdomen, feeling the strength of the contraction and looking at the clock. 'They seem to be coming more frequently, Sally. How do you feel about that pool?'

'Let's go for it. But not until you've told me about Patrick. You met him in America, had sex and it was completely amazing and that's why you're here.'

Hayley's eyes widened. 'Are you clairvoyant?'

'No, I'm a woman.' Sally reached for her bag. 'Patrick is unreasonably sexy. If I'd met him when I was single, I would have slept with him too. But don't tell Tom that. I need Patrick conscious until this baby is born. On the other hand, he might be the one to floor my Tom—he's strong enough. Mmm…' She gave Hayley a wicked look. 'So—I haven't actually seen him naked but it's got to be a good sight. Am I right?'

Hayley was laughing, her face scarlet. 'Sally, for goodness' sake…'

'Oh, please indulge me, Hayley. I feel like a whale and I'm in pain and scared. I need distraction.'

Hayley saw something flicker in Sally's eyes and she leaned forward and hugged her impulsively. 'Don't be scared,' she said huskily. 'You're going to be fine. We're going to do it together.' Wondering whether she'd overstepped the mark, she pulled away, but Sally yanked her back again.

'Don't stop. You have no idea how good it feels to be hugged. Tom is so stressed he's forgotten to hug me. But don't think that's going to get you off the hook. I still want to know everything. We've all been longing for Patrick to find someone.'

Hayley straightened. 'Don't get the wrong idea.' Hayley reached for the set of scrubs that Maggie had given her. 'It really isn't like that.'

Sally's eyes narrowed. 'But you'd like it to be, obviously. And he couldn't stop looking at you when he was in here earlier.'

'Really?' Startled by that piece of information, Hayley felt her stomach curl and then she shook her head. 'I don't know what to think. He wasn't that thrilled to see me.'

'Hold that thought—contraction coming.' While Sally breathed steadily, Hayley struggled to hold back the sudden surge of happiness that engulfed her like a cloak. Had he been looking at her? Really?

Now that the shock of her arrival had faded— *now that he knew she wasn't pregnant*—was he pleased she was here?

'Hey, no dreaming unless it's out loud.' Sally poked her in the arm and gave a faint smile. 'You're depriving me of a vicarious sex life, I can feel it. Tell me every little detail. You know you want to.'

And Hayley discovered that she *did* want to. So she told Sally everything.

'And you just left his room? You didn't even

wake him up?' Sally clutched her arm. 'I think I might be ready for the water.'

'Let's get you over there now.'

'Wait a minute.' Sally winced. 'Has he given you your knickers back?'

Hayley blushed. 'He hasn't mentioned them.'

'Probably too much of a gentleman.'

Hayley thought about the way he kissed. 'I don't think he's that much of a gentleman.'

'Ooh, don't tell me that—you're making me all hot.' Sally laughed, reaching for her bag.

'I'll carry that.' Hayley took it from her and together they walked across the corridor to the room where the birthing pool had been prepared. 'Don't say anything to him, will you?'

'And risk upsetting him? You're kidding aren't you?' Sally eyed the pool. 'That sexy man of yours is the only thing that's standing between me and a Caesarean section. I don't know what's wrong with Tom. He doesn't usually intervene so readily. With me he just wants to yank it out and get it over with. I suppose it's the whole control thing.'

Hayley helped Sally change into a swimsuit and step into the bath. 'How's the water?'

'Perfect, thanks. I wonder what Patrick has done with my husband?'

'I think he knew you needed time to calm yourself down, without having to worry about him.'

'Possibly.' Sally slid into the bath. 'Oh, my goodness, that feels fantastic. I should have overruled Tom ages ago when he said he didn't want me in water.'

'Why doesn't he want you in water?' Hayley checked Sally's temperature and recorded it in the notes. 'Has he had a bad experience or something?'

'He's fine with other pregnant women using the pool.' Sally closed her eyes and leaned back against the side of the pool. 'Just not me. As I said, he just wants to get this baby out as fast as possible. Poor man. I don't think this is going to be fast. Which brings me to another issue— you're not even supposed to be working, and neither is Patrick.'

'I don't mind.' Hayley poured Sally a drink. 'Here. You have to drink plenty while you're in there—I don't want you getting dehydrated.'

'It's Christmas Day. You could at least have provided champagne.'

'That comes after you've delivered the baby.' Hayley saw Sally's expression change. 'You're having another contraction?' She waited for the contraction to end and then listened to the foetal heart with the aqua Doppler.

'That sounds loud and strong.' Patrick strolled into the room, with Tom hovering behind him. 'Do you mind me in here, Sally? I have seen you in a swimming costume before.'

'Please don't tell me husband that.'

Tom dropped into a crouch by the pool, his expression contrite. 'I'm sorry I've been an idiot.'

'It's all right.' Sally leaned forward and kissed him, her eyes soft with love. 'I'll find a way to make you pay, you handsome thing.'

Tom looked up at Patrick. 'You won't give her systemic opioids while she's in the pool, will you?'

Patrick rolled his eyes. 'Do I look stupid?'

Tom ran his hand over the back of his neck. 'Sorry.'

'I thought I'd calmed you down,' Patrick said wearily, and his colleague gave a sheepish smile.

'I'm not going to be calm until this child is at university. Probably not even then.'

'In that case, I want a divorce,' Sally said, and

Hayley tensed, wondering whether Patrick would be sensitive about that comment, but he was busy checking the notes she'd made.

'This looks good.' He flicked through the pages and glanced at her. 'You're thorough, aren't you?'

'She's amazing,' Sally murmured, holding onto Tom's shoulders as another contraction ripped through her. 'I'm so glad you brought her in, Patrick. She's the best Christmas present you could have given me.'

Tom scowled, but his hand was gentle as he smoothed Sally's damp hair away from her face. 'Since when has my colleague bought you Christmas presents?'

'Since he was my colleague, too.' Sally groaned and leaned her head against his shoulder. 'I worked with him until six months ago, don't forget. That was when you were still sane, by the way.'

'You worked here?' Startled, Hayley put down the aqua Doppler that she'd been using to check the baby's heart rate. 'Are you a doctor?' *Please don't say she'd been giving advice to a doctor for the past few hours.*

'Sally is a midwife.' Tom looked at her and Hayley gave a whimper of embarrassment.

'You're a midwife? Why didn't anyone tell me? I had no idea.'

'I'm not a midwife at the moment,' Sally murmured. 'I'm a pregnant woman and, believe me, it's entirely different. You can see that just by looking at my husband. Normally he's a cool, calm professional but today he's turned into a psycho freak father-to-be.'

'Thanks,' Tom said dryly, offering his wife another sip of water. 'It's just because I care about you.'

'Please don't get sentimental.' Patrick gave a mock shudder. 'I prefer it when the pair of you row.'

'No. No rowing.' Sally gritted her teeth again and dug her nails into Tom's arm. 'It was a row that put me in this position.'

'Actually, it wasn't so much the row as the making up,' Tom drawled, and Patrick backed towards the door, shaking his head.

'Enough! Hayley and I will leave you to be romantic for a few minutes.'

Agreeing that the couple needed some private time, Hayley checked the foetal heart once more before following Patrick. But before she left the room she cast a final glance towards Sally. 'Everything is fine. I'll be back in ten minutes but if you're worried, press the buzzer.'

Patrick pushed coins into the vending machine and bought two cups of hot chocolate. 'I'm not asking you what you want.' He handed one to Hayley. 'You'll just have to trust me when I say that the tea tastes like dishwater and the coffee tastes like battery acid. Hot chocolate is the only option.'

'Hot chocolate is good.'

'You must be exhausted—let's go and sit in my office for five minutes.'

She followed him into the room and looked around. 'Where are the children?'

'They've gone down to the play area outside the children's ward. Posy likes the rocking horse.' Patrick gestured towards the armchairs. 'Collapse for a minute, I'm sure you need it. I can't thank you enough for everything you're doing for Sally.'

'Oh…' She blushed and sipped her chocolate. 'It's my job.'

Her job.

Patrick lounged in his chair, realising that he'd

never given any thought to Hayley in her professional capacity. In fact, he was embarrassed to admit that most of his thoughts about her had been of a much shallower nature. 'You're a fantastic midwife. Tom isn't easy to deal with but you stood your ground with him and you calmed Sally down. And she isn't easy. She's very exacting.'

'There's nothing wrong with being exacting.'

'That's why she's so relaxed with you—your attention to detail is incredible.' He looked at her curiously. 'You don't know this department but in no time at all and with no apparent fuss you've located every piece of equipment you need, every request form and observation chart—it's all done. Perfect. I could stand up in a court of law and produce evidence of perfect care.'

Hayley looked alarmed. 'I hope you won't have to stand up in a court of law because of anything I've done. In my experience that sort of thing only happens when there's a breakdown in communication.'

Patrick grinned. 'And that's another thing you excel at—communication. The aromatherapy was a good idea. Who taught you to do that?'

'I went on a course. I think relaxation is important for a pregnant woman. I used to run relaxation classes in Chicago and I often used aromatherapy on the unit.' She blew gently on her drink to cool it. 'I don't believe childbirth is all about following the textbook. It's about doing what works for the individual, isn't it? That might not be aromatherapy or massage. A few weeks ago I had a woman who couldn't bear to be touched so massage was out of the question.'

'So what did you do with her?'

'I found out what she usually did to relax.' Hayley took another sip of her chocolate. 'Turned out she liked listening to story tapes. So that's what we did. Instead of playing music, we listened to an actor reading Charles Dickens. I quite enjoyed it, actually. Made a nice change.'

Patrick lifted his eyebrow. 'You got to the end of the book?'

'It was a long labour,' Hayley said cheerfully, and Patrick looked at her with new respect, realising how little he knew about her.

Away from the work environment she was funny and self-deprecating, but here she was pure professional. 'Did you always want to be a midwife?'

'It was that or paediatric nursing but I found

that too upsetting,' she admitted. 'Midwifery is a happy job.'

Patrick laughed. 'A *happy* job?'

'Yes.' She gave a self-conscious shrug. 'You get to spend time with people in their happiest moment and I think that's very special. There is no feeling as good as handing someone their child, is there? Of course, sometimes it goes wrong and that's dreadful.' She paused for a moment and he sensed there had been plenty of moments in her career that hadn't been 'happy'.

'And then there's the long hours.' Patrick thought about the moans of the midwives he worked with. 'Missing weekends.'

'But that's because, generally speaking, you're staying with a woman right the way through her labour, and that's wonderful.' Hayley put her cup on the floor. 'The alternative would be handing over care to someone else halfway through labour. I think that's unfair on the woman and stressful. You have a short time in which to build a relationship of trust—you can't go home halfway through and expect that woman to just bond with someone else.'

'So you're not tired of midwifery?'

'Tired of it? Gosh, no. Never. I love it. Perhaps I haven't done it for long enough to become disenchanted.'

Patrick watched her curiously. It was so unusual to hear someone saying how much they loved their job. But Hayley was so enthusiastic he could imagine she'd lift the spirits of any colleagues she worked with. And he couldn't imagine her becoming disenchanted with anything. 'You must love it,' he drawled softly, 'or you wouldn't be here on Christmas Day.'

'You gave me no choice.' But her smile said otherwise. 'What about you? Don't you love it?'

'Yes. Although occasionally I worry about my children. Inevitably I'm called out more than I'd like to be.'

'How do you cope with child care? I would have thought you'd have a live-in nanny.'

'I didn't want someone living in our home,' Patrick said quietly. 'I wanted it to be just us. A family. But it's harder that way—requires more planning. Posy comes to the nursery in the hospital—that's easy. Alfie goes to school. And I use Mrs Thornton before and after school. And she stays the night occasionally if she has to.'

Hayley grinned. 'This is the same Mrs Thornton who wears scary red lipstick and fancies you?'

Captivated by her smile, Patrick had to force himself to concentrate. 'That's the one. She's actually very good with the children. And she's relatively local, which helps. Although clearly I have to make sure I'm not alone in a room with her.'

Hayley looked at him. 'Well, I'm sure it's hard, juggling work with children, but you obviously thrive on it. You look very happy for a man who's working on Christmas Day.'

Did he?

Patrick gave a start. He *was* happy, he realised. *Very happy.* Just being around her made him want to smile. That realisation unsettled him. 'It's Christmas Day,' he said blandly, standing up and throwing his cup in the bin. 'And my friends are about to have a baby. Plenty to smile about.'

Hayley stood up too. 'Christmas babies are always exciting.' Her eyes sparkled and Patrick suddenly wanted to box her up like a present and keep her in his life for ever.

Seriously spooked by his thoughts, he dragged his gaze from hers and pushed open the door.

'Come on. We'd better get back before Tom has a nervous breakdown.'

Over the next few hours, Hayley stayed with Sally, monitoring mother and baby.

'Tell me I'm making progress,' Sally moaned, and Hayley smiled and dimmed the lights slightly.

'You're making excellent progress. I'm proud of you.' As she finished speaking the door opened and Patrick strolled into the room.

'Hi, there. Just checking up on you.' Patrick squatted down next to Sally and touched her arm. 'How are things?'

Hayley's heart was bumping so hard she turned away and concentrated on the charts to give herself a moment to recover.

'I'm never sleeping in the same bed as Tom again if that's what you're asking me.' Sally breathed in deeply. 'And I want Hayley to come and live with me and be my new best friend. Apart from that, everything is fine.'

Realising that if she didn't respond she'd draw attention to herself, Hayley turned with a smile. 'I'll come and live with you. You make me laugh and you have the same size feet as me. I can borrow your shoes.'

Patrick glanced at Tom. 'You're looking tense. What's the matter?'

'I want her out of the water,' Tom muttered, but Sally rolled her eyes and Patrick stood up and took the charts from Hayley.

'This is looking fine.' He scanned them carefully. 'Remind me how long she's been in the water?'

Hayley checked the clock. 'Four hours.' She lifted her eyebrows. 'That went quickly.'

'It's because we were talking about the three S's.' Sally tightened her grip on the side of the pool. 'Shoes, shopping and sex.'

'Sex?' Patrick's eyes narrowed and he turned to look at Hayley, a question in his eyes.

She tried to look innocent but felt her cheeks growing hotter and hotter under his sharp blue gaze.

He knew. He knew she'd been talking about him.

Oh, help—couldn't Sally have been a little more discreet?

'Nothing like a conversation about sex to remind a girl how she got herself in this mess,' Sally said blithely, and Hayley squirmed.

'I think I'll just get myself a quick drink as the two of you are here.' Desperate to escape, she pushed the aqua Doppler into Patrick's hand and slunk towards the door. 'Back in a minute.'

CHAPTER FIVE

HAYLEY hunted down somewhere to hide her burning face. Why had Sally been so tactless? *What on earth was she going to say to Patrick?* She wished she hadn't been so honest with Sally. Slinking along the corridor, she found a staffroom. Fortunately it was empty, several half-drunk cups of cold coffee abandoned in the middle of the table.

New Year's resolution, she told herself firmly. No more talking about herself. Ever.

'So whose sex life were you talking about?' Patrick's voice came from behind her and she spun round nervously.

'Oh, I thought you were with Sally.'

'Tom's with Sally. Despite his apparent ineptitude he is, in fact, more than capable of monitoring his own wife for ten minutes.' Patrick's gaze didn't shift from her face. 'So?'

'So, what?' Keeping her tone innocent, Hayley avoided the subject, hoping he'd just give up. 'Sally's lovely, isn't she?'

'Delightful. She's also extremely preoccupied with my love life.'

'She cares about you. Do you want tea? Coffee? No, of course you don't. You want to get back to Sally.' She looked at him pointedly but he didn't move.

'How much did you tell her?'

Hayley looked around desperately, wondering if the staffroom had an emergency exit. She had a feeling she was going to need it. *What had Sally said to him?* She tried to buy herself some time, hoping that his mobile would ring. 'What makes you think I told her anything?'

'Hayley.' Patrick's voice was patient. 'There is a taxi driver a few miles from here who knows everything about you from your bra size down to the colour of your knickers, and you were only in his vehicle for fifteen minutes. You've been with Sally for the best part of six hours so I think it's fair to assume that she has a fairly good grasp of your life story by now.'

'I did *not* tell him the colour of my— That was

a total accident because he just happened to pick the phone up when I was talking to you and that was *absolutely* not my fault.' Affronted, Hayley looked at him but still his gaze didn't shift from hers and she scowled. 'Did you ever think about being a lawyer? You should be a lawyer. You have a way of looking at people that makes them want to confess to things they didn't do. Could you stop looking at me like that?'

Patrick's brows lifted, but there was a glimmer of humour in his eyes. 'How am I looking at you?'

'Like I'm an idiot,' Hayley mumbled, and the humour faded.

'Hayley, I do not think you're an idiot. Far from it. On the contrary, I think you're an exceptional midwife. *Really* exceptional. Sally isn't an easy patient and you've got her eating out of your hand.'

'That's different.' Hayley stopped the pretence of making tea. 'That's my job. But the rest of it— I feel guilty,' she admitted hopelessly. 'And, yes, I feel like an idiot because I should have been able to find some way of smoothly deflecting her questions, instead of which I just blurted everything out like I always do.' She gave him a look of helpless apology. 'Why do I always do that? Why can't I just be discreet and enigmatic?'

'I'm not sure if that was a rhetorical question but if you really want an answer then I suspect it has something to do with the fact that you're incurably honest.'

'Well, whatever it is I am, I wish I was something different.' Frustrated with herself, Hayley flopped down onto the chair and buried her face in her hands. 'I'm *so* sorry. I messed up. I admit it. I didn't *want* to say anything, I didn't want to embarrass you, but Sally sort of wormed it out of me and if I hadn't answered I would have looked rude. She's a patient and a consultant's wife and anyway she sort of guessed and—'

'Hayley, breathe.'

'Sorry?' She glanced up at him and saw that the humour was back in his eyes.

'As usual, you're forgetting to breathe. You're going to pass out.'

'I never pass out. I've never fainted in my life.'

'Then let's not make today the first time.'

'Look, I feel really guilty, OK? I mean, this is where you work.' Nervous under his steady gaze, she pulled the clips out of her hair, twisted it and pinned it up again. 'And I can understand that you don't want people gossiping about you. I'm *really* sorry I told her.'

'In the interests of consistency, what exactly did you tell her?'

'The truth, of course.'

Patrick studied her for a moment, a strange look in his eyes. 'How much of the truth?'

'Enough. I mean, I didn't tell her absolutely *everything*—' Hayley frowned, trying to remember exactly what she *had* said. 'I definitely missed out the part where you thought I was pregnant and I skirted over the bit where you kissed me in the kitchen.' Her face burned at the memory. 'But I might have mentioned one or two things about that night in Chicago.'

His face was poker straight. 'Did you tell her that you left your knickers on my bedroom floor?'

Hayley squirmed. 'Maybe. Possibly. It might have been mentioned.'

The corner of his mouth flickered. 'It sounds to me as though you've been the soul of discretion.'

'You're laughing at me again.'

'I'm not laughing. Hayley you're so sensi-tive—'

'Because I know I keep saying the wrong things at the wrong time! I just can't stop myself. My mouth is constantly getting me into trouble.' She heard him draw in a breath and saw his gaze drop to her mouth and linger there as if he was thinking about…

And so was she.

She was thinking about nothing else. *Sex, sex, sex.* That was the only thing on her mind when she looked at Patrick.

Hayley jumped up and hurried over to the water cooler, wondering whether she could fit her burning body inside it. She'd made a decision that she wasn't going to think about him in *that way.* And now she was doing it again. One look, and she was willing to forget all her promises to herself. Really, she needed to do something about herself. Something serious.

'So you're not mad with me, then?' Keeping her tone light, she poured herself a glass of water that she didn't want.

'I'm not mad. But I did want to check exactly what you've told her so that we give her the same story.' Patrick joined her at the water cooler and gently removed the cup from her hand, his fingers brushing against hers. 'Do you mind if I drink that, given that you don't want it?'

'How do you know I don't want it?' Her voice was a squeak and his eyes gleamed with gentle mockery.

'Because you're easy to read.' His eyes rested on hers for a moment and then he sighed. 'I think perhaps it's time I took you home.'

Hayley's heart pounded like the drum in an orchestra.

He wanted to take her home? Oh, God, yes. Right now. She wanted to try out his enormous bed with the view over the forest. She wanted to see if he could repeat the magic he'd created that night in Chicago.

Staring up at him, her legs wobbled. *His eyes were so blue,* she thought dreamily—so blue it was like staring into the Caribbean ocean. Lost in a fantasy that involved herself and Patrick on a white sandy beach, it came as a shock when he frowned urgently.

'Hayley? You need to decide. Is it yes or no?

No one is going to judge you. I'll take you if you want me to.'

She felt a thrill of shock at his unapologetically direct approach.

He wanted her that badly?

'Gosh, Patrick, I— You make it really hard for a girl to stick with her decisions, I'll give you that.' But the fact that he was so desperate for her he just wanted to take her home *right now* sent excitement pouring through her body. Flustered, she tried to disengage her eyes from his. How was she supposed to think when he was staring down at her with unflinching concentration, as if she was the only thing in his world? 'I mean it is flattering, obviously, that you feel this way. And I'm not pretending I'm not really tempted— I mean you *know* I am because I already left one pair of knickers in your room.' She fiddled with her hair. 'But the sensible side of me is saying that we ought to give this a bit more thought this time. I suppose what I'm saying is that frankly I'm surprised you even want to take me straight home given what happened last time. I mean, you didn't contact me, I contacted you. And then you thought I was pregnant—'

He looked taken aback. 'Hayley—'

'I know, I know.' She lifted a hand to silence him. 'That was all a misunderstanding, but still I think it should remind us both that we have to think about this. Not jump in with both feet. Yes, there's chemistry. I'm not denying that. But that doesn't mean that we have to do something about it.' *Who was she kidding?* If they didn't do something about it soon she was going to go screaming mad. Her body was melting, her pelvis was on fire and all she wanted him to do was kiss her the way only he could kiss. 'I'm just saying I think it might be a mistake. Not that I'm not flattered that you asked, of course—'

'Hayley.' His expression hovering somewhere between stunned and incredulous, Patrick ran his hand over his jaw. 'I was asking whether you wanted to go home.'

'I know, I heard you, and I still think that—'

'Because it's late. I thought you might be very tired.' He spoke the words slowly, emphasising each one as if she were a small child. 'You're jet-lagged. I thought you'd need some rest.'

Rest?

He was suggesting that she go home to *rest?*

Facing the onset of massive embarrassment, Hayley looked at him stupidly. 'You want me to— You were suggesting— Oh.'

There was a shimmer of amusement in his eyes, but also a flicker of sympathy. 'Hayley, listen, don't for one moment think that I don't—'

'If you laugh now, Patrick Buchannan, you will never be able to deliver a baby again,' she warned huskily, 'let alone make another one of your own. If you laugh, you will never again have to ask a woman if she's pregnant.'

'I'm not laughing.'

'Good.' She lifted her chin, trying to hold onto the last shreds of her dignity, trying to look as though this situation was entirely normal and that she didn't really want to die on the spot. But she saw immediately that this whole misunderstanding was her fault. Because she'd been thinking about nothing but sex, she'd assumed he'd be the same.

'Right. So you were, in fact, asking whether I want to go home and sleep.' Hayley cleared her throat and tried to make her voice sound casual. As if she had conversations about sex every day of the week. As if she were a twenty-first-century woman. 'Of course. That's fine.' *This was even*

more embarrassing than realising she'd left her
knickers on his bedroom floor.

'Hayley—'

'It's kind of you to offer, but actually I'm not
particularly tired.' She felt like a stripper who
had accidentally turned up at children's party. 'I
don't need to go back to the house now.' She was
never going back to his house again. As soon as
the shift was over she was going to change her
identity and leave the country. Maybe she'd
become a nun—at least that way she wouldn't
have the opportunity to proposition men.

'You've done us a favour, coming in,' Patrick
said cautiously, watching her closely as if he was
afraid she might flip at any moment. 'You've
calmed Sally down, it's probably because of you
that she's progressed. But none of us are forgetting it's Christmas Day and you weren't supposed
to be working. The night staff will be here soon.'

'Sally is only eight centimetres dilated. I won't
leave until she has the baby.' And that would
mean staying near to Patrick. *Oh, Hayley, torture*
yourself, why don't you? Still, if things got too
bad she could always drown herself in the
birthing pool. 'I'll stay.'

'You're sure?'

'Oh, yes. I'm very good at decisions. Once I've made a decision...' Hayley snapped her fingers '...that's it. Done. I never change my mind.' *Well, only about three thousand, two hundred and fifty-four times.*

'That's very generous of you. Sally will be relieved—and so will Tom. He rates you, and that's a compliment coming from Tom.'

Now he was flattering her to make her feel better, Hayley thought gloomily, remembering the sympathy in his eyes. He must think she was a sad, desperate woman. Not wanting to dwell on that, she changed the subject. 'What are you going to do about the children? It must be Posy's bedtime.'

'It is. If you're sure you're willing to stay for Sally, I'll send the kids home with my brother. They won't complain—they adore Daniel.'

'So you're not going to ring the babysitter with the vampire lipstick?'

A sardonic smile flickered across his handsome face. 'I think we might give her a miss this time. I think spending Christmas night with a vampire might be a little unfair on the kids.

Although I have asked her to pop in and check on the kittens.' His eyes gleamed with irony. 'Yours and mine.'

'I love the kittens.' Why did he have to be so good-looking? It wasn't fair. Things would have been much easier if he'd been small, earnest and academic. Reminding herself that if he'd been small, earnest and academic, she wouldn't have left her knickers on his bedroom floor, Hayley smoothed her scrub suit and tried to look professional. *As if she hadn't just made it obvious that her feelings about him were anything but professional.* 'I'd better get back before Tom has a breakdown. You go and sort out the kids.'

'Alfie advertised for a housekeeper? And he used my credit card?'

'Yes, but that will teach you to leave it lying around.' Patrick handed his brother a large bag. 'This is everything they're going to need for the night. You know, it might be easier if you just stayed in our house—'

'No.' Daniel gave a strange smile. 'Today I asked Stella to marry me—'

'I know.'

Daniel's brows rose. '*How* do you know?'

'You're forgetting I have Alfie. He knows everything that goes on around here,' Patrick said wearily. 'So, did Stella say yes?'

'Of course she said yes.'

'Then she's a brave woman.'

'She is brave. Brave and beautiful.' A strange look crossed Daniel's face. 'I never thought I'd feel this way, to be honest. Never thought I'd have the courage—never thought I'd feel this way about a woman.'

Patrick opened his mouth to deliver the usual onslaught of brotherly banter but the words wouldn't come. Instead, he found himself thinking of Hayley. 'I'm pleased for you,' he said gruffly. 'And I'm sorry I'm giving you the children tonight. You must be looking forward to romance.'

'Stella is thrilled to be having the children,' Daniel said dryly. 'You know what she's like.'

'Yes. You're lucky.'

At that moment Stella bounced through the doors, her eyes shining. 'Patrick! Has he told you our news?'

'Alfie told him our news,' Daniel drawled, and Stella giggled. She was about to speak when the door opened and Hayley entered.

'Oh—I'm sorry. I didn't know you had anyone with you.' She coloured prettily and would have left but Patrick beckoned her into the room.

'Hayley, this is my brother, Daniel, and Stella—his wife-to-be. The children are going to stay the night with them. Guys, this is Hayley—she's Alfie's housekeeper. And she just happens to be a midwife, too.'

'She worked in America, isn't that a coincidence?' Alfie was bouncy and cheerful. 'You should taste her turkey, Uncle Dan. I want Dad to keep her for ever. No more gluey pasta. No more burnt everything.'

Hayley's face grew scarlet and she busied herself retrieving Posy's toys from the floor. 'I'm just here for two weeks, Alfie.'

Patrick's eyes lingered on the curve of her bottom as she stooped. Then he started thinking about the tiny pair of silk knickers he'd found on the floor of his hotel bedroom…

Dragging his gaze from her curves, he discovered his brother watching him with amusement.

'You look hot and bothered, Ric.' Daniel's eyes gleamed wickedly. 'Something wrong?'

'It's always difficult juggling kids and work,' Patrick said smoothly, and Daniel's grin widened.

'Well, we're taking the kids off your hands for a night, so that should make things easier for you.'

Apparently oblivious to the byplay, Hayley zipped up the bag and Alfie hugged her.

'Tomorrow can we play Monopoly? I want you to stay longer than two weeks, Hayley. Promise you will.'

'Well, no…' Flustered, Hayley hugged him back. 'I can't do that, Alfie, but—'

'I know.' Alfie looked crestfallen. 'You have to track down the friend you met when you were in America.'

Seeing Hayley's stricken expression, Patrick intervened. *She'd had enough embarrassment for one day.* 'Alfie, get your things together. Posy needs to get to bed.'

'It's Christmas night, Dad. It doesn't matter if she's late.'

'If she's late she'll be cranky in the morning.'

Patrick felt Stella's eyes on his face, questioning. Clearly Alfie's unguarded comment hadn't passed unnoticed.

Damn. He wasn't ready to field her questions—*didn't know what his answers would be.*

'So…' He took the bag that Hayley had packed and thrust it towards Daniel. 'I'm sure you want to go home and I have to get back to work.'

'You were supposed to be off over Christmas,' Stella murmured, and Patrick shrugged.

'Sally went into labour.'

Stella gasped. 'No. Really? I must go and see her for a minute. Which room is she in?'

'She's in the water.'

'That's what I came to talk to you about.' Hayley pushed her hair behind her ears. 'Tom wants her out of the water, but she's refusing.'

Patrick wondered if she knew she always played with her hair when she was nervous. 'I don't want her to deliver in the water either. I'm with Tom on that.'

Stella rolled her eyes. 'Obstetricians unite. What do you think, Hayley?'

The door opened again and Tom stood there, panic on his face. 'She wants to push, Hayley. And I can't get her out of the water.'

Patrick noticed that his colleague immediately turned to Hayley. She'd gained his trust over the hours she'd been with them. And that didn't surprise him. She'd gained his trust, too. There was no doubt in his mind that she was an exceptional midwife. Even now she didn't panic. She kissed Alfie briefly, congratulated Daniel and Stella again and then walked briskly back along the corridor with Tom, talking quietly and calmly.

'I've got to go.' Patrick thrust slapped his brother on the shoulder and kissed Stella. 'Thanks, guys.'

Having hugged his children, he followed Hayley and Tom along the corridor. When he opened the door he sensed the change in the atmosphere. Tom was beside himself and Sally was pushing. In the water.

'Please, angel.' Tom was white-faced. 'Out of the water.'

'If you move me now, I'll kill you,' Sally gritted, screwing up her face as another contraction hit her. 'Oh, God, Tom, how could you do this to me? It's agony!'

Tom looked stricken and Hayley touched his shoulder gently. 'This is part of labour,' she said softly. 'Don't take it to heart.'

Patrick had entered the room, prepared to find ways of persuading Sally out of the water, but, watching Hayley, he held back.

'What do you want me to do?'

'Nothing.' She gave Sally another sip of water. 'You can stay around and give Tom some support.'

Patrick caught his friend's desperate look. 'There's no reason why she shouldn't deliver in the water, Tom—'

'We don't do that.'

'Not normally,' Patrick agreed. 'But Hayley has delivered babies in the water, and it's what Sally wants. And to be honest, it's too late to get her out. Let's go with it. I'll be right here all the time. If there's a problem, I'll intervene.'

'Thanks for being so positive,' Sally groaned, and Patrick grinned.

'I'm an obstetrician. What do you expect?'

'Oh, go and get a coffee or something.' Sally grabbed Hayley's hand. 'I don't want this to be unsafe and I'm not thinking clearly. What do I have to do? I want you to tell me everything. I don't want you to assume I know anything.'

'You're doing fine.' Hayley waited for another contraction to come and go and then checked the foetal heart. 'The baby is fine, too. Don't push, Sally, not unless you have the urge.'

'Just get the baby out,' Tom muttered, but Hayley ignored him, all her focus on Sally.

'You're doing so well. The head is nearly out, Sally. So now we've come this far, the baby needs to be born under the water. And I'm going to be as hands-off as possible because that's best for both of you.'

Tom looked as though he was going to pass out, but Patrick was fascinated.

He watched as Hayley calmly soothed Sally, offering encouragement and guidance but in such a low-key way that it appeared that she wasn't helping in any way. But Patrick saw the skill in what she was doing.

'I want to push,' Sally groaned, and Hayley nodded.

'Push, then.'

Realising how rarely he saw calm, normal deliveries, Patrick felt a lump build in his throat as Sally and Tom's baby was born into the water with a minimum of fuss.

Hayley brought her gently to the surface and into Sally's arms.

'Congratulations. You have a daughter.' The baby gave a little wail and then Sally was crying and when Patrick looked at Tom he saw that his colleague's face was wet.

'Congratulations,' he said huskily, and Tom pressed his fingers to his eyes and then bent to hug his wife.

'You clever, clever girl.'

Smug and proud of herself, Sally glanced up from admiring her daughter. 'You see? Sisterhood. We women can do it without you.'

Hayley grinned. 'Actually, we could do with their help to get you out of the pool now, Sally. Then we can clamp the cord and cut it.' She reached for a towel and gently dried the baby. 'We need to keep her warm.'

As Hayley calmly checked the baby's Apgar score and finished the delivery, Patrick found himself watching her work.

'I've never witnessed such a calm delivery,' he said softly, and she smiled as she tucked the baby up warmly against Sally's breast.

'It's the way it's supposed to be.'

'Only *without* the water,' Tom muttered, and Sally grinned.

'I told you I wasn't going to get out of the water.'

'I thought you were joking. If I'd known you were serious I would have made you give birth in the middle of a desert.'

'Everything looks fine, Sally,' Patrick said quietly, 'but, given that you delivered under the water, I'd like a paediatrician to check the baby.'

'I'd like that too.' Sally smiled at him. 'Thank you for letting me do it. Thank you for not panicking and thinking about your legal position.' She turned to Hayley, her eyes misting. 'And thank you for making it all so special. When I have my next baby, I want you there.'

'Next?' Tom was incredulous, his expression comical as he dragged his hands through his already untidy hair. 'Sal, a moment ago you were saying never again.'

'That was then and this was now.' Sally's happiness was infectious. 'I want lots of babies, Tom.'

Patrick grinned. 'And she wants them all underwater.'

CHAPTER SIX

IN THE car on the way home, Hayley shut her mouth tightly and kept it shut. Once or twice she felt Patrick glance towards her but she kept her eyes straight ahead, staring at the snow that swirled across his headlights.

He seemed unconcerned by the horrendous weather conditions, his hands firm and confident on the wheel as he negotiated the snow and ice. 'You were amazing with Sally.'

'Mmm.'

'Is that all you're going to say? "Mmm"?' His tone was amused and she sneaked a look at him and then immediately regretted it as her body responded in its usual predictable fashion.

She concentrated her attention back on the snow.

Was it normal to feel like this about a man? After her outburst earlier he was probably terrified to be alone with her. The situation was so embarrassing it made her squirm.

She shifted slightly to the far edge of her seat so that she was as far away from him as possible.

'Hayley, you're worrying me.' He eased the four-wheel drive through the gate and pulled up in front of the barn. 'Are you ill? Tired?'

Actually, she *did* feel tired. Bone-achingly weary, but that was hardly surprising, was it?

'I'm fine.' They were the only words she allowed herself but he gave a sigh and switched off the engine.

'You're upset about earlier.' With the engine off the cold immediately penetrated the car and he looked at her profile for a moment and then sighed. 'Come on. We can talk inside.'

Hayley Hamilton, you are not talking, she reminded herself fiercely. *You are not saying a word. Nothing.*

She slid out of the car, took a moment to balance herself and then Patrick put his arm round her and guided her to the door. And she couldn't pull away because she knew that any sudden movement was guaranteed to land her flat on her back on the ice.

So she endured the warmth and strength of his arm but still kept her mouth zipped shut.

Even when he closed the door on the cold Christmas night, she didn't move her lips.

Instead, she hurried across to the dining table, which was still covered in empty plates and abandoned crackers.

'What are you doing?' Patrick watched as she noisily stacked plates and scooped up jokes, toys and paper hats. 'Leave that.'

'I'll just take it through to the kitchen,' she said brightly, balancing a stack of plates and walking away from him.

'In that case, I'll help you.' The muscles in his shoulders flexed as he removed his coat. 'It will be quicker if two people do it.'

'I don't want you to help! I'm the house-keeper. This is my job.' She disappeared into the kitchen, hoping that he wouldn't follow. She wanted to be left alone with the washing-up and her humiliation.

But he didn't leave her alone. 'You've also worked all day as a midwife,' he said mildly. 'We'll do it together, Hayley.'

Together.

Why did he have to use that word? She was trying not to think 'together'.

'Fine.' She hurried back to the table, horribly conscious that it was just the two of them in the barn—horribly conscious of the width of his shoulders and the way he kept looking in her direction.

Swiftly she gathered glasses and after several trips to the kitchen the beautiful contemporary dining area was once more clear. Patrick had turned on the Christmas tree lights and chosen a CD. A female with a sexy, smoky voice sang about love and loss and Hayley returned to the kitchen, clattering as loudly as possible to drown out the soulful notes.

'I've never known you so quiet.' He stood in the doorway, a concerned look on his face. 'What's wrong?'

Oh, for goodness' sake! How could he ask her that? *What's wrong?*

Wasn't it obvious?

She gritted her teeth and finished loading the dishwasher. 'Nothing is wrong.'

'Is this about what happened earlier?'

'Of course not. Why would you think that?'

'Hayley, you have no reason to feel embarrassed.'

'Of course, no reason at all.' Hayley crashed the door of the dishwasher shut and set it to rinse. 'It isn't embarrassing to proposition a man at work. It happens to people all the time.'

'You didn't proposition me.' His tone was mild. 'You thought I was propositioning you.'

'Thanks for reminding me of the details. I'm well aware that I misread the situation, but do you mind if we don't talk about this?'

'And I would have been propositioning you if the wife of my closest friend hadn't been on the point of delivering and my children hadn't been across the corridor.'

'I really think we should just—' She broke off and stared at him. 'What? What did you just say?'

'I said I would have been propositioning you. You didn't misread the situation, Hayley. I was worried that you were tired, that's true. I thought you might want to hand Sally's care over to another midwife and get some rest, that's true as well.' His tone was soft. 'But I want you as much as you want me.'

'Oh…'

'And I've already missed the cut-off point for a four-minute warning, so I'm giving you about…' he glanced at his watch '…three seconds.'

'Three sec—' The words vanished under the pressure of his mouth and Hayley moaned as his tongue traced her lips, sending shock waves of excitement through her body. She had no idea how he'd crossed the room so quickly, but as his hands slid into her hair and his mouth grew more urgent on hers, she didn't care.

He powered her back against the table, his hands biting into her thighs as he lifted her up and lowered her onto the surface. A mug toppled and smashed on the kitchen floor, but neither of them noticed. Hayley was incapable of noticing anything except the hot burn of sexual desire in Patrick's eyes. The fact that he wanted her so badly increased her own desperation and she gave a whimper of need and arched her hips, but he was already there, his hands unzipping her jeans and stripping them from her legs.

His breathing was uneven as he brought his mouth back down on hers, his kiss so disturbingly erotic that Hayley's mind blanked. Heat pooled in her pelvis and she tried to shift against him, instinctively trying to relieve the delicious burning that had become her entire focus. The dangerous throb and ache became so intense that she sobbed against his mouth and he muttered something against her lips and then slid his fingers inside the elastic of her panties.

His touch was unerring, his fingers so impossibly skilled that Hayley was left in no doubt that he knew more about her body than she did. Without warning she exploded in a climax that made her cry out in shock, the sound muffled by his mouth, every contraction intensified by the fact that his fingers were deep inside her. His mouth still on hers, he gently removed his hand and Hayley was dimly aware of him altering her position slightly— and then there was a brief pause before she felt the hard probe of his erection against her hot, molten core. He entered her with a smooth, decisive thrust, the strength and power of his body robbing her of breath. And he felt so shockingly good that she arched her hips, responding to the rhythm he set. His mouth stayed hot on hers, his body virile and demanding as he slid his hand under her hips, hauling her closer still, increasing the contact that was already driving both of them wild.

Neither of them spoke—not a word was exchanged—all communication channelled through their bodies and expressed through the ragged drag of their breathing.

When he finally lost control Patrick's hands tightened on her hips. His rhythm altered and that subtle change was sufficient to boost Hayley over the same precipitous edge until both of them were tumbling, spinning, falling through a kaleidoscope of sensations.

Hayley had long since lost track of time but eventually Patrick dragged his mouth from hers and dropped his head to her shoulder, his breath warm against her neck. 'That was…' His voice husky, he struggled to finish his sentence. 'Sublime.'

She lay there, too drugged to move, her body still trembling. It was only when he shifted above her that she felt the hardness of the kitchen table pressing into her back.

Patrick registered her wince of discomfort with a wry smile of apology. He hauled her upright in a decisive movement and scooped her into his arms as if she weighed nothing.

Hayley wound her arms round his neck. 'You'll do yourself an injury.' Eyeing her jeans on his kitchen floor, she wondered whether she was destined to leave clothes in every room this man inhabited.

'You don't weigh anything.' He took the stairs that led to the bedrooms, pushing open the door that led to his room. As he laid her down on the bed, Hayley realised that he was still wearing his coat.

'One of us has the dress code wrong,' she muttered. 'Either you're wearing too much or I'm wearing too little.'

'We're both wearing too much,' he drawled, his eyes glittering like sapphires as he shrugged off his coat and reached for the buttons of his casual shirt.

Her mouth dried. 'Patrick—'

'Hayley?' The shirt went the same way as the coat and his fingers slid to the snap of his jeans.

Her eyes were on his board-flat abdomen and then he was on the bed beside her. Reaching out, he dimmed the lights and then pulled the duvet over both of them. 'Now—where were we?'

Hayley lay still in the darkness, feeling the warmth of his arms around her. He hadn't bothered to close the blinds in the bedroom and tiny lights glowed like stars in the fir trees outside the barn. Through the thickness of the glass she could hear the dull roar of the beck as it raced down from the fells.

'You're very quiet.' Patrick's voice was low and masculine. 'What's wrong?'

'What makes you think there's anything wrong?'

'Because normally you don't stop talking,' he said dryly, curving her against him in a possessive movement. 'I've learned that when you're quiet, it's time to worry.'

'That isn't true.' She resisted the temptation to snuggle into him and heard him sigh.

'Hayley, I can tell there's something wrong. Do I have to put the lights on and interrogate you?'

'I'm fine, Patrick, really.'

'Why are we whispering? We're on our own in the house. Apart from the kittens, of course, and I don't suppose they're interested in us.'

His words hastened the deflation of her happiness. It was like going from a slow puncture to a blowout, she thought miserably. Her emotions crashed and with it her desperate attempt to keep her feelings to herself.

Hayley shot out of the bed but his arms caught her easily and he pulled her back.

'Leave me alone, Patrick,' she muttered, her voice thickened by tears she desperately didn't want to shed.

'Hayley, now you're really worrying me.' His voice concerned, he flicked on the bedside lamp and shifted above her, his eyes fixed on her face. 'Tell me what's wrong.'

'I just hate myself, that's all.' Hayley turned her face away from the light, aware of the tension in his powerful frame.

'You hate yourself? For spending the night with me?'

'Yes!'

Her confession was followed by a long silence and then she heard his slow, indrawn breath. 'Did I hurt you?'

'No.' Her face was burning and she wished she'd stayed silent or given him a neutral response to his original question. 'It was fine. Can we just forget it?'

His fingers slid around her face and he forced her to look at him. This time there was no trace of humour in his eyes. Just serious intent. 'Hayley, don't avoid this—I thought it was what you wanted. Was I wrong?'

'No, you weren't wrong! Of course I wanted you—that must have been pretty obvious to you from the moment I dropped my knickers on your bedroom floor the first time.' Her voice rose slightly. 'And I wasn't exactly fighting you off tonight, was I? So it's a little unfair of you to rub in the fact I can't say no to you.'

His eyes were wary. 'I didn't want you to say no to me. So what's the problem?'

'The problem is that you only ever do this when your children aren't around—when I turned up yesterday, or the day before yesterday or whenever it was…' She realised that she'd lost track of the time. It must be the early hours of the morning, which meant it was no longer Christmas Day. 'When I turned up, you looked at me with the same enthusiasm you would have shown a tax bill. Almost the first words you say to me are, "When is the baby due?" Then at the hospital you're very remote and distant and suddenly we arrive home and just because the house is empty you turn back into a rampant sex god—' She broke off with a moan as he covered her mouth with his, kissing her slowly and thoroughly until the fire in her pelvis flared to life again.

When he finally lifted his head she was dizzy and disorientated.

'We need to talk,' he said softly, curving his hand around her face. 'You're right—I haven't behaved well where you're concerned. Give me the chance to explain.'

'You don't need to explain.' Hayley tried to wriggle away from him but his weight kept her still. 'Honestly—just forget I said anything. It's my fault, I know. Other women have one-night stands all the time and have no problem with it—I'm just built wrong.'

'You're built perfectly.' There was a sardonic gleam in his eyes as his gaze lingered on her mouth and then drifted lower. 'And I do have things to tell you. Things you deserve to know.' He rolled away from her and sat up. 'Can I get you anything? Are you hungry? We haven't eaten since lunchtime.'

Hayley realised that she was *starving,* but she wanted to hear what he had to tell her. Was it about his ex-wife? 'I'm not hungry.' But her stomach chose that moment to growl in protest and she rolled her eyes as he laughed.

'Not hungry?' Springing from the bed, he

strolled into the bathroom and emerged wearing a black robe. 'I'll go and put some food on a tray. I'll be back in a minute. I've put the bath on. I thought your muscles might ache after all that…activity.'

Avoiding the glitter of his eyes, Hayley waited for him to leave the room and then slid out of bed and padded towards the door he'd used.

Seeing his bathroom, she felt ever so slightly faint. It was huge. Huge and super-luxurious in a cool, contemporary style, with a walk-in shower and what seemed like hundreds of tiny lights in the ceiling. But the real luxury was his bath. It was easily big enough for two. Water cascaded into the tub and mixing with the scented bubbles he must have added before he'd left the room.

As the water level rose quickly, Hayley looked at the bath longingly. Maybe a bath was a good idea.

Just a quick one.

She slid into the water and closed her eyes with a moan of pleasure.

'I didn't know what you wanted to eat so I made a few different things.' Patrick's voice came from inside the bathroom and Hayley opened her eyes with a shocked squeak.

'What are you doing in here?' She noticed that the tray he was carrying contained a bottle of champagne as well as a stack of thick-cut sandwiches.

There was a dull popping sound as he removed the cork from the champagne. 'I thought this would be a good place to eat. That way we don't get crumbs in the bed.' He poured champagne into two glasses and handed her one. 'Merry Christmas.'

'Merry Christmas,' Hayley said weakly, watching as he placed the tray next to the bath, discarded his robe and stepped into the water next to her. 'When you suggested a bath, I didn't know you were going to be joining me.'

'Why not?' He gave a slow, sexy smile and drank from his glass. 'Have something to eat. I'm not much of a cook, as you've been told, but I can just about manage sandwiches. Turkey, of course. No surprise there.'

'I love turkey sandwiches,' she said truthfully, reaching for one and biting into it. 'I really am starving.'

'I'm not surprised. It was a long day. Sally and

the baby are fine, by the way. I called when I was downstairs.'

'I'm glad.' Hayley was tense with anticipation, wondering what he was going to tell her. 'I love your bathroom. I could move in here for the rest of my life.'

Patrick gave a faint smile. 'My wife hated it.' He glanced around the bathroom. 'She thought it was too modern.'

'Really? I think it's gorgeous. Like being in a smart hotel. I'm waiting for you to give me a bill when I step out of the door.' Hayley lay back against the side of the bath. 'I feel as though I'm in a Hollywood movie.'

'I don't think they usually eat cold turkey sandwiches in Hollywood movies.' Patrick watched with amusement as she devoured another sandwich and she shrugged.

'Jet-lag always makes me hungry.'

He lifted an eyebrow. 'Jet-lag?'

'Well, OK.' She felt her cheeks redden. 'It's entirely possible that the sex had something to do with it—maybe—just a little.' She watched while he put his glass down, sensing that he was deciding exactly what to tell her. 'I wish I could be more like you. I mean, I can see you carefully planning what to say and I just can't do that! I have all these plans to keep my thoughts to myself and then they sort of tumble out of my mouth.'

'I'd noticed.' He smiled at her and lifted the bottle of champagne but she shook her head.

'I'm already tired. If you give me any more I won't wake up until January.' She hesitated. 'You don't trust me enough to tell me, do you?'

'It isn't about trust,' Patrick said evenly. 'It's more about not wanting to relive it, if I'm honest. You already know some of it. You know that my wife— ex-wife—left on Christmas Eve two years ago.'

'Yes.' But she didn't know *why*. And she wanted to know why. 'The poor children. And poor you, of course,' she added quickly, but he shook his head.

'No. Your first reaction was the right one. I'm a grown-up, I can look after myself, but Alfie and Posy…' After a moment's hesitation, he topped up his own champagne glass, watching as the bubbles rose to the surface. 'If Carly had cared more about their feelings, she might have handled the situation differently. But she didn't. She was angry with me and she didn't care that they suffered.'

'Why was she angry?'

'Because I wasn't who she wanted me to be.' Patrick's tone was devoid of emotion, his eyes strangely blank. 'She thought she'd married a high-flying obstetrician. When I was made a consultant her words were, "Now I've made it." At the time I thought she'd made a mistake and what she'd meant to say was, "Now you've made it." But, no, she really did mean that. For her it was all about social status. She pictured herself walking into smart dinner parties with me—the problem is that obstetricians are probably the most unreliable guests on anyone's list.'

'You were always working.'

'Of course. In fact, you could say that there was an inverse correlation between the growth of my career and the decline of my marriage. The more successful I was, the busier I became. I started to see patients from all over the country and because some of the work was challenging, I couldn't always delegate.' Patrick gave a humourless laugh. 'In business, inappropriate delegation leads to lost revenue—in obstetrics it's a dead baby or a dead mother. And that's a no-brainer as far as I'm concerned.'

'Couldn't she understand that?'

'Carly wasn't interested in my work—just in the concept of being married to a successful consultant. But there's not much point in being married to a successful consultant if he's so busy working he can't take you anywhere. She was bored.'

'She had the children.'

Patrick gave a cynical smile. 'As I said, she was bored.'

'Did she have a career of her own?'

'When I met her she was working as a secretary to my colleague—I was a registrar. She didn't want a career. She wanted a successful husband.'

'You fell in love with her?'

'Honestly?' Patrick put his empty glass down. 'No. That wasn't what happened. I thought she was pretty. I asked her out a few times—'

Hayley gave a soft gasp of understanding. 'Oh, no, she became pregnant—and you married her.'

His blue eyes narrowed. 'Astute, aren't you?'

'Not particularly—but it explains why your first thought when you saw me on your doorstep was that I must be pregnant.' She stared down at the bubbles in the bath, absorbing that new information. 'No wonder. No wonder you thought that.'

'The crazy thing was Carly and I didn't even really have a relationship—not a proper one. I'd taken her out to dinner twice and on that last occasion she invited me in for coffee.' Patrick dragged his hand over the back of his neck and shrugged. 'She told me she was taking the Pill and on that one occasion I wasn't careful—'

Hayley remembered how he'd always used condoms with her. *Always been careful.* 'So you married her.'

'And we were happy enough, or so I thought.' Patrick shrugged. 'She wanted a big house—I gave her a big house; when she said Alfie was hard work, I paid for her to have help. I did my best to turn up at dinner parties, although I confess I rarely managed to stay through three courses. There were lots of occasions when I worked through the night—you know what it's like. But we muddled through—and then we had Posy.' He closed his eyes briefly. 'It went downhill from there.'

'Why?'

'Because Carly nearly died in childbirth,' he said hoarsely, 'and she blamed me. I think her exact words were, "*You save every other bloody woman but you're going to let me go because I'm not good enough for you.'"*

Hayley winced. 'What happened?'

'I don't know,' Patrick said wearily. 'I wasn't doing the delivery for obvious reasons—we were having a nightmare in the department, staff off sick, too many difficult deliveries in one night. Carly was in labour, but everything was fine—routine. And then there was a real emergency and I had no choice but to leave Carly and perform an emergency section on this lady. And I was only just in time—we would have lost that baby if I hadn't operated when I did. But while I was gone Carly started to bleed heavily.'

'Oh, Patrick…'

'The midwife was from another hospital and she panicked—I suppose because she knew Carly was the wife of a consultant. There was a delay. By the time I returned to the room it was horrendous. I thought we were going to lose Posy, so in the end I took over charge of the delivery—I couldn't trust anyone else at that point. And I had no choice but to do a Caesarean section.' He pulled a face at the memory. 'If I'd been there all the time—monitored her—I might have been able to do everything differently.'

'And another woman's baby might have died,' Hayley said softly, tears in her eyes. He'd performed an emergency Caesarean section on his own wife—to save the life of his own baby. 'You must have nerves of steel to have been able to do that.'

'I had no choice. To be honest, I blocked it out. I didn't let myself think, This is my wife, my baby.'

'Patrick, that must have been so hard. You had to make decisions that no man should have to make.'

'Carly didn't see it that way,' Patrick said roughly. 'She thought I'd let her down, and maybe I did—I don't know. I go over it in my head again and again. What didn't I see? What did I miss?'

'You didn't miss anything,' Hayley said quietly. 'I'm sure of that. You're a brilliant obstetrician.'

'But a lousy husband,' Patrick said softly, and Hayley shook her head.

'No. You were put in an impossible position. But I don't understand why Carly was so upset. If she knew the other lady would have lost her baby…'

'I think she just panicked and I wasn't there,'

Patrick said wearily. 'And when I was there I was focused on saving her and Posy, not on stroking her arm and telling her I loved her. In fact, I pretty much ignored her emotional trauma at the time—I just didn't want her to bleed to death or Posy to die. But I see now that I made it much, much worse. If Tom or one of the others had been on duty it would have been different, but you can't be an obstetrician and a husband at the same time.'

'That's why you sacrificed your Christmas day to help Tom and Sally.'

Patrick leaned back against the bath and closed his eyes. 'I just know what it's like trying to play both roles—and it's not good. Anyway, Carly was furious about the section—she hated having a scar.'

'Having seen the way you work, I doubt she had much of a scar.'

'It was more than she could cope with.'

'Wasn't she relieved that you'd saved Posy?'

'If anything, she saw that as more evidence that I didn't care for her.' Patrick opened his eyes and looked at her. 'The one thing I didn't tell you was that she got pregnant on purpose that first time—she confessed as much to me after one too many glasses of wine one night. She was shocked it only took once, but thrilled with herself. She said that all she ever wanted was to marry a doctor. But the reality wasn't what she expected and she became more and more unhappy.'

'Did you love her?'

Patrick hesitated. 'I adored the children, and she knew that. She always said I only cared about the children. I used to try and get back from the hospital in time to bath them and put them to bed, and then I'd go back to work again and sometimes stay out all night. It's hardly surprising my marriage collapsed.'

'She has to take responsibility for it too,' Hayley said stoutly. 'She forced you into that position.'

'I shouldn't have married her, but that was just one of many mistakes I made with Carly, the first being the fact I took her to bed in the first place,' he said wearily. 'My second mistake was trusting her to take care of contraception—I take full responsibility for that. It was carelessly irresponsible of me, but I can't feel too sorry about it because if it hadn't happened, I wouldn't have Alfie.'

And she knew how much he adored his son.

'So what happened two years ago? Why did she suddenly walk out?'

Patrick gave a short laugh. 'It was a pretty memorable Christmas. Daniel proposed to Stella on Christmas Eve and we all opened a bottle of champagne and Carly had made an elaborate celebration lunch. Just as she put it on the table—'

'Your phone went and you had to go to the hospital?'

Patrick gave a faint smile. 'How did you guess? There was no way I could delegate it. This lady was having triplets and I was concerned about them.'

'Triplets? Wow.' Hayley slid closer to him. 'I've never delivered triplets. Sorry, go on.'

'When I arrived back from the hospital there was a taxi in the drive and Carly was waiting by the door with her bags packed. She'd already told the children she couldn't live with me any more.'

'Oh, God, Patrick, no.' Hayley's heart ached at what that must have done to Alfie, who would have been old enough to understand. 'And that was it? What about access? Seeing them?'

'She doesn't see them,' Patrick said coldly. 'Don't ask me why.'

Hayley tried to imagine a woman not wanting

to see her children but failed. 'Do you think it's because she loved you so much she just had to make a clean break?'

Patrick gave her an odd look. 'That's the generous interpretation,' he said softly, lowering his head to kiss her gently. 'I don't think that. I think she wanted to start afresh and the children would have held her back. If you want my honest opinion, I'm not sure she ever really wanted children. I think they were just part of the life-style package she wanted for herself. An acqui-sition. Like a new kitchen,' he said wryly, 'only more work.'

Hayley felt a surge of outrage on his behalf. 'So you were left on your own on Christmas Eve—'

'Actually, no.' Patrick turned the hot water on again. 'Daniel was so freaked out that Carly had walked out, he broke off his engagement to Stella and he walked out, too.'

Hayley stared at him in disbelief and Patrick shrugged.

'Daniel and I had a very dysfunctional child-hood. It was like living in a war zone most of the time. Dan was always nervous about marriage. In fact, it was an indication of just how much he

loved Stella that she even got him to propose—
and if Carly hadn't walked out that night they
might have stayed together and not have wasted
two years.'

'It scared him?'

'It reminded him that relationships are difficult, fragile things. So Stella and I were left on
our own, both of us crushed.' He gave a faint
smile. 'Unbelievable, really. Anyway, we joined
forces that Christmas and put on a giant act, as
you do when you have children—and somehow
we got through.'

Hayley slid deeper under the warm water. 'So
for two years you concentrated on your children
and then you met me—and you thought you'd
made the same mistake again.'

'No.' Patrick's tone was rough. 'I never thought
that. What you and I share is entirely different
and it has been from the first moment.'

'But I can see why you must have been so
worried. Your children's lives have been shat-
tered and you've just got things back
together—and then I arrive. And you thought I
was pregnant. You were worried I'd expect you
to marry me.'

Patrick sighed. 'I admit I'm a bit sensitive to that issue. I overreacted.'

'And I can understand why.'

Patrick took her face in his hands. 'I'm glad you came, Hayley. I'm glad you stayed. Alfie already adores you. I've never seen him take to anyone so quickly.'

'Thank you for telling me the truth,' Hayley said softly. 'And for what it's worth, I don't think pregnancy is a reason for marriage either. My dad married my mum for the same reason and it was a disaster. There's no love there. Never was. And my step-siblings really resent me and always have. It hasn't made for a happy family.'

'I can see why you didn't want to spend another Christmas with them.'

'I wanted to find *you*. I wanted to know whether what we'd shared was all in my imagination.'

'It wasn't in your imagination.'

'When you opened the door on Christmas Eve I wanted to die on the spot. All I kept thinking was, *I got this wrong,*' she confessed. 'I wanted to melt into a snowdrift. I realised then that for you it had just been a one-night stand.'

'That wasn't how it was and you didn't get it

wrong—although I admit that seeing you on my doorstep was a shock.' Patrick stepped out of the bath and tugged a huge warm towel from the heated rail. 'That night in Chicago took me by surprise. I hadn't been with a woman for a long time. That should tell you something about the way I felt.'

Hayley followed him out of the bath and took the towel he offered her. 'Desperate?'

He made an exasperated sound and brought his mouth down on hers. 'Smitten,' he said against her lips. 'I was smitten, you silly girl.' He scooped her up again. 'But I was desperate, too.' He strode back into the bedroom and tumbled her onto the bed, the damp towels falling onto the floor. As he stroked her hair away from his face, his eyes were suddenly serious. 'I'm glad you came, Hayley. You have no idea how glad.'

'I thought you were panicking.'

'I never panic.' He wiped a droplet of water from her face. 'But I was worried—for all the reasons I just explained.'

'Well, I'm not pregnant, so you can relax.' Hayley stifled a yawn, thinking that she'd never felt so tired in her life.

Patrick pulled her into his arms. 'You poor thing—first jet-lag then a day at work and then—'

'Fantastic sex,' Hayley said sleepily, a grin on her face. 'Don't apologise for that bit.'

She was already drifting off as she felt him pull her into his arms. 'Sleep,' he said quietly. 'And tomorrow we can have some fun with the children.'

CHAPTER SEVEN

'So MUCH for not working over Christmas.' Maggie handed Patrick a thick set of notes. 'What are you doing for New Year? Are you treating yourself to a night off?'

'Maybe. Depends on this place, doesn't it?' Patrick frowned at the list on his computer screen, careful not to reveal his plans for New Year's Eve. He was taking Hayley out. *They were going to have some time on their own.* 'Why is this clinic so busy?'

'Because everyone who was trying not to see you over Christmas now wants to see you.' Maggie was looking at him expectantly and Patrick lifted an eyebrow.

'What?'

Maggie grinned. 'You were right. She's very pretty. And fun.'

'*Who* is very pretty and fun?'

'Hayley, of course.'

'You fancy Hayley?'

'Patrick Buchannan, you are *not* going to change the subject.'

'I wasn't aware that I had.' Resigning himself to the inevitable, Patrick sighed. 'Go on, then. What do you want to know?'

'Is it serious between you?'

'She's my housekeeper, Maggie.'

'I've seen you looking at her, Patrick.'

'Obviously, I look at her.' Patrick kept his tone casual. 'She's worked every shift here for days.'

'It isn't the fact that you look at her it's the way you look at her. You're clearly crazy about her,' Maggie said happily. 'And she *adores* you, anyone can see that. And I just love happy endings.'

Patrick ran his hand over his jaw. 'Maggie, there is no happy ending—it's too soon. We haven't even…' *What?* What hadn't they done?

Spent time together.

Their relationship had been intense and concentrated and he knew better than anyone that sex was no basis for a long-term relationship.

But it wasn't just sex, was it?

The more he discovered about her, the more he liked and admired her.

Maggie folded her arms. 'I've known you for seven years. I knew you when you went through the trauma of Posy. I even made you tea when Carly left you. I deserve to enjoy the good bits with you.'

It was just the reminder he needed. 'Given that my wife walked out two years ago, I'm not likely to jump into another relationship in a hurry.'

'Your relationship with Carly was over a long time ago. And if something is right, it's right,' Maggie said stoutly. 'You don't need decades to know it's right.'

'Hayley arrived a week ago. A week!'

'But you met her a few weeks before that.'

'We spent one night together that's all.' Patrick dropped his pen on the desk and exhaled sharply. 'Why am I discussing this with you?'

'Because I love you. And because I deserve some excitement in my life. What about Alfie and Posy? The children like her, I'm sure. She's such fun.'

Patrick had a mental image of Hayley playing hide and seek through the barn the day before. Alfie had been Robin Hood, Posy tripping over a long dress as Maid Marion and Hayley had been the wicked Sheriff of Nottingham. He smiled slightly at the memory. 'The children adore her.'

Maggie gave a wistful sigh. 'That's wonderful, Patrick. I'm so pleased for you. At last you've found someone.'

Patrick sent her a warning glance. 'Don't. I'm taking this slowly, all right? I'm not going to make another mistake.' *At least she wasn't pregnant.* That took the urgency out of it. They had no need to make any quick decisions about anything. They had time to let their relationship develop. He was going to take her out. 'If it works, great. If it doesn't, we'll part company.'

'You'd better not part company. She's a fantastic midwife, I can tell you that.' Maggie glanced at her watch. 'We're quiet on the labour ward so I've brought her down here to help you in clinic.'

Patrick greeted that news with mixed feelings. 'You think I'm going to feel romantic in clinic?'

'No, but the only other available midwife is Sandy and she's so in love with you she can't concentrate. Hayley actually seems to manage to be in love with you and still get her work done.'

'Oh, for goodness' sake.' *She was in love with him?* Patrick frowned. No. Of course she wasn't.

'And you care for her, too. I've never seen you as happy as you've been over the past week. Marry her, Patrick,' Maggie advised. 'Don't hesitate.'

'Maggie, I barely know her. She's been over here for less than a week.' *And it had been the most frustrating week of his life.* Apart from Christmas night when they'd been on their own without the children, they'd made a point of staying away from each other. And abstinence was driving Patrick nuts.

'Right. Enough of this.' Striving to hold onto his sanity, he changed the subject. 'Anything going on upstairs that I ought to know about?'

'Katie King's blood pressure went up so she's fed up because she knows you won't be sending her home.'

'She's right. I won't.' Patrick sat back in his chair. 'What else?'

'Vicky Thomas has gone into labour. She came in last night.'

'Vicky? Why didn't anyone call me?'

'Because you deserve the odd evening at home with your family,' Maggie said mildly. 'Tom sorted her out last night. He said he owed you that one. He adjusted her insulin. He said he was going to call you to discuss it.'

'He didn't. No doubt he's in new father mode. All right—I'll go up and see her when I've finished clinic. What about—?' Patrick broke off as someone tapped on the door and opened it.

It was Hayley, wearing the dark blue scrub suit that all the midwives wore, her dark hair fastened haphazardly in a twist at the back of her head. 'I'm sorry to interrupt you—I've just seen a woman who is thirty-six weeks and I'm worried about her. She says she has flu—she's been ill over Christmas.'

'Another one?' Maggie sighed and walked towards the door. 'The Lake District is simmering with germs at the moment. I still have three midwives off sick.'

Patrick was looking at Hayley, trying to keep his mind on the job. 'You're worried?'

'Yes. I don't think it's flu.'

'What are her symptoms?'

'Vomiting, epigastric pain, headache, shivering.'

'Vomiting? Could be norovirus,' Maggie murmured, but Hayley shook her head firmly.

'It could be, but I don't think it is. Her face is swollen, and she looks…' Hayley shrugged. 'I don't know—I just have a bad feeling. I think she could be showing signs of pre-eclampsia.'

Maggie checked the list in her hand. 'What's her name? Who is her consultant?'

'She isn't local. That's the other reason I'm worried. She told me that she was checked in clinic just before Christmas. They told her that a certain amount of swelling is normal, but her ankles are so bad she's having to wear her husband's slippers.'

Patrick stood up. 'She's staying up here?'

'With her family over Christmas. And in the last week she's put on 4.5 kilos.'

'It *is* Christmas,' Maggie said cautiously. 'I haven't dared stand on the scales myself, but I'm willing to bet that—'

'No.' Hayley interrupted her with a brisk shake of her head and Patrick found himself wondering how she could be so confident in her work and so under-confident in the rest of her life.

But that was the impact of her step-siblings, he thought, knowing only too well what damage family could do.

'I know it's Christmas,' Hayley said, 'but I've questioned her carefully and she hasn't eaten much—she's been feeling too ill.'

Patrick was already by the door. 'Blood pressure?'

'She says it's been "high normal" for the past two months but the hospital didn't seem to think there was any reason to worry. It's 140 over 100.'

'Urine?'

'Trace of protein.'

'I'll take a look at her before I start clinic. Maggie, do we have an antenatal bed should I need one?'

Maggie sighed and pulled her notebook out of her pocket. 'Yes, because Tom is going to discharge his twins lady this morning once Paeds have checked the babies.'

'Good. I'll let you know if I'm going to need it.' Patrick followed Hayley out of the door and into the next room.

'Charlotte, this is Patrick Buchannan, the consultant.' Hayley picked up the notes and handed them to Patrick. 'Charlotte carries her own notes.'

'Which is helpful.' Patrick scanned the notes, picking out the information that he needed.

'Hayley, there's no record of a platelet count from the day assessment unit—could you call them and see if they did one? It might just not have made it into the notes.' He listened as Charlotte outlined what had happened, and by the time she reached the end of her story Hayley was back.

'They only do it on new hypertensives.'

Patrick glanced at the blood-pressure reading in the notes but decided not to worry Charlotte by verbalising his thoughts. 'All right, so we'll start fresh. I want to do an ultrasound now, and then I want to do a full blood count and check liver function and renal function.' While Hayley fetched the ultrasound machine, Patrick turned back to the woman on the bed. 'I agree with Hayley—I don't think this is a virus.'

Charlotte exchanged glances with her husband. 'But I saw my GP in London before I left and he just said there was a lot of it around—everyone is ill.'

'That's true,' Patrick said carefully, 'but in this case it's something different.'

'You think it's the baby?'

'Yes, I do. Have you heard of pre-eclampsia?'

Charlotte shook her head. 'No.'

'It's a condition that occurs only in pregnancy and it causes a number of changes in your body, including high blood pressure and a leakage of protein into your urine.'

'But I felt fine until just before Christmas— surely it's more likely to be a bug?'

'In its early stages it has no symptoms, but as the condition becomes more serious a woman is likely to experience changes—for example, headaches, stomachaches, vomiting, sometimes visual disturbances.'

Charlotte stared at him. 'I saw flashing lights for a short time yesterday evening.'

Patrick kept his expression neutral. 'Right. Well, that might be related. The swelling may also be related.'

'My doctor told me that no one takes any notice of swelling now—that it's normal for pregnant women.'

'It can be normal,' Patrick agreed, preparing the ultrasound machine. 'But it can also be a sign of problems. In fact, all those symptoms I just mentioned can be attributed to other causes, which is why the condition can be missed. I want to start by looking at the baby and the placenta,

Charlotte. Has the baby been moving?' As he performed the scan he kept questioning her, his eyes on the screen. 'All right, there's the baby's head—and his heart—and that's the placenta.'

Charlotte peered anxiously at the screen. 'It all looks like a squirmy mess to me. Does the baby seem all right?'

'The baby seems fine.'

Charlotte's husband cleared his throat. 'So how do you treat pre-eclampsia?'

'You can't treat it. You can manage it...' Patrick pushed the ultrasound machine away from the bed '...but basically the condition ends when the baby is delivered.'

'But I have another month to go!'

Patrick sat on the edge of the bed. 'Charlotte, you need to prepare yourself for the fact we may need to deliver the baby sooner than that. At thirty-six weeks, your baby is well developed and should have no problems at all. We have to balance all the factors.'

'All right. Obviously I want to do what's right for the baby,' Charlotte said nervously. 'So what happens now?'

Patrick stood up. 'I'm going to arrange for you

to be transferred to the labour ward. Then I'm going to do a series of tests and when I have the results I'm going to decide what the best course of action is. In the meantime, I'm going to give you something to lower your blood pressure and Hayley is going to stay with you and monitor both you and the baby.'

Charlotte's eyes filled with tears but before Patrick could speak, Hayley slipped her arm round Charlotte's shoulders and gave her a hug. 'You poor thing, this must be such a shock for you,' she said soothingly, 'but it will all be fine. I'm going to take you upstairs and make the room cosy, and we can have a good chat. You can tell me everything about your Christmas.'

She was so tactile, Patrick thought to himself as he stood up and picked up the notes. As sensitive with the patients as she was with his children.

'One of my team is going to come and take some bloods from you,' he told Charlotte, 'and I'll be up to talk to you later. Hayley, let's give her some labetalol.' He scribbled on the drug chart and handed it to Hayley, who followed him out of the room.

'You're worried too, I can tell. You're treating a borderline blood pressure.'

He gave a faint smile. 'I am. I'm sure my colleagues would frown with disapproval.'

'You think her condition is worse than it appears.'

'Yes, I do,' he said frankly. 'I think her blood pressure is going to rocket.' He heard her sigh with relief at his response and then she stood on tiptoe and impulsively kissed him on the cheek.

'I was afraid you might not take it seriously. That's what I love about you—I mean like,' she amended hastily. '*Obviously* I mean like, not love. What I *like* is that you follow your instincts and don't just rely on tests and machines.' She was delightfully flustered by her slip and Patrick wondered what she'd say if she knew that his instincts were prompting him to behave in a deeply unprofessional way. In fact, if he followed his instincts at the moment there was a strong chance he'd be arrested and struck off simultaneously.

Obstetrician interrupts busy clinic to have steamy session with midwife.

'We'll watch her for the next hour and see how she goes, but I'm ready to deliver that baby if it becomes necessary.' His eyes lingered on her face for a moment. 'You did well. It could easily have been a virus at first glance. What made you suspicious?'

'I'm hyper-sensitive to it. I've looked after a woman with eclampsia before.' Her eyes misted. 'We lost her, Patrick. The only time I've ever lost a patient. And she wasn't our patient—it was similar to this situation. She was visiting her sister in Chicago and she had a fit. It was awful. Truly awful. That poor father, the baby…'

Patrick reached out and touched her shoulder and then wished he hadn't because the chemistry was instantaneous. He stepped back from her at exactly the same moment she stepped back from him. 'Take her upstairs and get her on a monitor,' he said roughly. 'I'm going to start my clinic and once the results are back I'll come and see her. But if there is any change, call me.'

Patrick arranged the tests immediately. While they were waiting for the results, Hayley settled Charlotte into the room, trying to make her comfortable.

'I wish Patrick Buchannan was my consultant,' Charlotte said as she flicked through a magazine that Hayley had given her. 'He's very ap-

proachable, isn't he? And gorgeous to look at—
not that I'm interested in that, of course.'

Hayley smiled as she checked the woman's
blood pressure once more. 'I should think you
have other things on your mind at this point.'

'Is he married?'

Hayley felt her heart miss a beat. 'No,' she said
carefully, 'he isn't.' And that meant he was free
to marry *her.* And no matter how hard she tried
to rein in her mind, she had an average of a
million fantasies an hour, all of which involved
her walking down the aisle towards him. He'd be
stunned by her beauty, of course, and for once
she was going to manage *not* to fall over—

'Hayley?'

'Sorry? What did you say?' Blushing, Hayley
pulled the CTG machine closer to the bed. 'I'm
going to monitor you for a while, Charlotte, is
that all right?' She must stop thinking about
marriage! Technically she'd known him for
about a week. And that one night, of course. But
that probably didn't count because they hadn't
done much talking. Either way, it had been a
short time. They needed to get to know each
other slowly, and maybe then—

'I asked you whether he's the sort of doctor who can't wait to do a Caesarean section.'

'No.' Hayley frowned. 'None of the doctors here are like that.'

Charlotte sighed. 'Back home I never see my actual consultant anyway. Every time I go it's someone else.'

'That happens sometimes.' Hayley didn't add that the 'someone else' who had seen her last time hadn't done their job properly.

'I wouldn't mind being one of Dr Buchannan's patients.'

'Mr Buchannan.' Silencing the wedding bells in her head, Hayley adjusted the machine. 'He's a surgeon, and we call surgeons Mr.'

'Oh—yes, of course. I knew that. I think.' Charlotte shifted slightly on the bed, looking at Hayley anxiously as the sound of the foetal heart pulsed around the room. 'Does that sound all right?'

'Sounds good.' Hayley checked the trace and then Charlotte's blood pressure.

'So how long have you worked here?'

'Actually, I arrived just before Christmas. Before that I was working in the States.'

'Oh. Are you here for good?'

Was she?

She hadn't actually given any thought to the future. Technically her job as their housekeeper was going to come to an end in a few days but no one had mentioned her moving out. And she couldn't imagine living anywhere other than High Fell Barn.

Perhaps the children would slowly just get used to the idea that she lived with them and from there it would be a natural progression for her and Patrick to get together.

Hayley was about to indulge in another brief wedding fantasy when Charlotte suddenly went rigid and started to fit.

'Oh, God, no, don't do this to me,' Hayley muttered, slamming her hand onto the crash button while supporting Charlotte to make sure she didn't fall off the bed.

The door swung open and Maggie ran in. 'What's happened?'

'She's fitting,' Hayley gritted, turning Charlotte onto her left side and reaching for the oxygen. 'Call Patrick and the anaesthetist and I need some mag sulphate.'

'I'll get the trolley.'

Maggie ran out of the room but she was back moments later and Patrick was with her.

Attaching Charlotte to a pulse oximeter, Hayley didn't even question how he'd arrived so fast. 'Her sats are 96.'

'How long has she been fitting?'

'Two minutes.'

'Let's give her a loading dose of 4 grams of mag sulphate. Have we got an infusion pump?'

They worked as a team, slick and professional as they tried to control the seizure.

'Foetal bradychardia,' Maggie said, watching the trace, and Patrick nodded.

'As soon as she's stable I'm going to do a Caesarean section. Gary?'

'Yes.' The anaesthetist was monitoring Charlotte's airway and breathing. 'Let's do it. Who is the next of kin?'

'Her husband, Andrew,' Hayley said. 'But he's just gone to phone his sister. They were staying with her over Christmas.'

'I'll go and sort out consent,' Patrick said, and Gary glanced at him.

'Didn't she show any early signs?'

Patrick checked Charlotte's patellar reflexes. 'Yes, although some of her readings were borderline. Her blood pressure was never quite high enough to ring alarm bells. But they ignored mild proteinurea, which wouldn't have happened in my unit.'

Gary lifted an eyebrow. 'Are you going to call them?'

'Yes.'

Surprised by Patrick's unusually terse tone, Hayley glanced at him and realised that he was really angry.

'Hayley is the hero of the hour,' he said quietly. 'She spotted it in clinic.'

Embarrassed to suddenly be the focus of attention, Hayley blushed and the anaesthetist smiled.

'Can we offer you a permanent job?'

'Oh— Well…' Hayley gave an embarrassed laugh, aware of Patrick's swift glance, but she was spared the trouble of answering by the arrival of Patrick's registrar and the rest of the team.

It was only later—hours after Patrick had safely delivered a baby girl and Charlotte was stable— that she had time to think about that remark.

A permanent job?

Stay here—permanently?

With Patrick. And his gorgeous children…

'Hayley?' One of the other midwives put her head round the staffroom door. 'Mr Buchannan wants you in his office. I don't know what you've done, but you'd better start thinking up your excuses. He looked serious.'

'OK, thanks.' Sure that she'd handed over Charlotte's care without missing anything out, Hayley walked to Patrick's office. Oddly nervous, she tapped on the door and walked in.

'You want me?' Oh, help, why did everything always come out wrong? 'I mean—I was told you wanted to see me?' Her cheeks were hot and he stood up in a fluid movement and strode towards her, slamming the door shut behind her with the flat of his hand.

'You were right the first time. I want you.' His mouth came down on hers and he kissed her with erotic purpose, his lips as skilled as ever as he aroused her to a state of screaming ecstasy in less time than it took her to gasp his name.

Desperate after several days when she hadn't been allowed to touch him, Hayley melted against him, his kiss muffling her gasp of shocked pleasure as his hands slid to her thighs.

'Patrick—' She tried to say that they probably shouldn't be doing this *here* but her mouth refused to do anything except kiss him back.

It was hot, desperate and frantic. When he stripped off the flimsy trousers of her scrub suit Hayley didn't protest, and when she felt him hard and ready against her, she gave a low moan and dropped her hands to his zip.

He entered her with no preliminaries but she was so ready for him it was as if they'd spent hours indulging in foreplay. And perhaps they had, she thought as her vision blurred. They'd been stepping around each other, trying not to do anything that would unsettle the children—trying not to touch.

But they were touching now. Hungrily. Ravenously seeking their fill of each other, their bodies joining in almost animal desperation. Overtaken by sensations so intense they were almost painful, Hayley felt her body reach its peak and he joined her in the same place, his strong fingers digging hard into her thighs, his mouth silencing her cries.

Breathless, her mind blank, Hayley dropped her head against his shoulder, and suddenly became aware of their surroundings. His computer screen flickered on the desk and somewhere in the distance she heard the wail of an ambulance siren.

'I've been wanting to do that all week.' Patrick's voice was low and rough and he scooped her face into his hands and kissed her gently. 'Sorry. It was a bit fast.'

'No problem,' she muttered faintly, her eyes on his mouth. 'Perhaps we can do it slowly, er, next time. When that midwife said you wanted to see me I thought I'd done something.'

'You have done something.' He kissed her again, his mouth lingering on hers. 'You've driven me wild. Living with you and not being able to touch you is starting to have an adverse effect on my mental health. What are the chances of you being able to sneak into my bedroom without the children finding out?'

'Sneaking isn't something I do well,' Hayley confessed as she adjusted her clothing. 'I have a habit of banging into things and falling over, remember? To sneak you have to be stealthy and graceful, and that isn't me.'

'I don't care.'

'Patrick you do care,' she said gently, glancing towards the door, relieved that no one had needed the consultant in the past fifteen minutes. 'You don't want to hurt or unsettle your children and neither do I.'

'No.' Patrick raked his fingers through his hair. 'So we'll do this slowly. Tomorrow I'm taking you out to dinner. You can wear a dress that I'm not going to remove and we'll have a conversation. I'll book a babysitter for the kids—'

'Can't we have dinner at home? Alfie hates Vampire Lips. I'll cook us something special and you can open a nice bottle of something from your cellar.'

Patrick shook his head. 'No. I want to spend some time with you without the children.'

'I love the children,' Hayley protested, and Patrick lifted his eyebrow.

'You don't want to be alone with me?'

'Of course I do.' She blushed. 'It's just that Posy looked as though she was starting a cold this morning so I don't want to leave her.'

He held her gaze for a long time. 'All right, this is what we'll do. If she's ill, we won't go out. But if she's fine, then I have a surprise for you. And you'll need to dress up.'

Hayley brightened. 'Dress up as in lipstick and heels? That sounds fun.' Happiness bubbled inside her as she reached for the door. It was going to be a lovely evening. He wanted time with her. He *liked* her. Life was perfect.

As she went back to the staffroom to change, she couldn't hold back her excitement. He hadn't mentioned that her contract was almost up. He hadn't suggested that she look for alternative accommodation. Far from it. He was as desperate for her as she was for him. And now he'd asked her to dinner.

Perhaps he was going to suggest that she just carry on living with them. They'd make plans for the future…

'Fabulous restaurant,' Hayley breathed. 'How on earth did you manage to get a seat right by the window? Don't tell me—you delivered the chef's baby.'

'Actually, yes. Have you met the waiter before?' Patrick watched as the blushing member of staff retreated to the kitchen.

'No. Never. But he was very friendly, wasn't

he?' Hayley took a sip of champagne and gave a low moan of pleasure. 'Oh, that tastes delicious. What a great idea to get a taxi so that we can have champagne.'

'Given that you're so intimate with our local taxi drivers, I'm surprised you didn't invite him to join us.'

'He wouldn't have wanted to. Jack's popping over to his daughter's for a few hours because she lives near here, but he'll be back to pick us up when we call.' She smiled at the waiter who was back with a basket of warm, freshly baked bread. 'Mmm. They smell good. I'll have the one with poppy seeds, please. Yum.'

The smitten waiter gave her two and Patrick managed not to smile until the man was safely back in the kitchen. 'Jack needs to watch out. I think he has competition. Maybe you shouldn't have worn that dress.'

There was a flash of insecurity in her eyes. 'You don't like the dress?'

'I love the dress,' he drawled. 'And so does every other man in the room.'

Her cheeks dimpled. 'Really?' She glanced down at herself self-consciously. 'Alfie liked it.'

'Alfie likes everything about you.' Patrick reached for his glass. 'To us.'

Hayley tapped her glass against his. 'To us.'

'Thank you for cooking us the best turkey we've eaten in years…' he kept his eyes on hers, unable to look away '…and for giving us such a happy Christmas.'

'I had a happy Christmas, too.'

'You didn't miss being with your family?'

Hayley took a sip of champagne and put her glass down. 'Families aren't always idyllic, are they? I used to hope that things would change as we all grew older but nothing ever did. I even tried changing myself to be more the way they wanted me to be, but it didn't work.'

'Why would you want to change?'

'Because I irritate them.' Hayley sat back as the waiter placed her starter on the table with a flourish. 'That looks delicious, thank you.' She beamed at him and Patrick watched as she picked up her fork.

'How could you possibly irritate them?'

'Just by being me.' She speared a prawn. 'I'm so different from them. They see me as a clumsy idiot who laughs too much and talks too much.

And they're probably right. But it's impossible for me to be silent and academic. I've tried. It doesn't work. And it's exhausting trying to be something you're not.'

'Don't put yourself down. The things you tried to change about yourself are the things that make you special.' He studied her across the table and found himself noticing new things about her— like the fact her eyelashes were long and dense and her lower lip was slightly fuller than her top lip. 'Aren't they proud of what you've achieved professionally?'

'They don't think I've achieved anything professionally.' Her voice was matter-of-fact. 'That's the point. They think I've wasted my life. They're always asking me when I'm going to get a "proper" job.'

Patrick felt a rush of anger towards her family. 'I think you've achieved tremendous success in your professional life.'

'It depends on how you define success, doesn't it?' She ate another prawn. 'Is success about making a difference to people's lives, or is it about how much money you accumulate?'

'Money isn't a measure of success so much as

an indication of career choice.' Patrick discovered that he'd finished his starter without even noticing that he was eating. 'If you pick a career like nursing or teaching you're never going to be rich, but that doesn't mean you aren't successful.'

She smiled at him. 'And that's why I'm eating dinner with you and not them,' she said lightly. 'Because you don't make me feel as though my entire life has been wasted.'

'Families can be tough.'

'Well, that's true. And from what you've told me, yours was no picnic either.'

They ate and talked and, by the time midnight arrived and the New Year had been toasted, Patrick discovered that he'd told her more about himself than he'd ever told anyone before. Certainly more than Carly.

Studying Hayley's smiling face as she told him a ridiculous story about one of her friends, he realised that comparisons with Carly were inappropriate.

There *was* no comparison.

When had Carly made him laugh like this? Had Carly ever asked if he should check his mobile phone in case there was a message from the hospital?

Aware that the restaurant had emptied and they were the last couple still talking, Patrick retrieved his phone from the pocket of his jacket and called the taxi, feeling nothing but regret that the evening had to end.

He wanted her to keep talking. He wanted to know *everything* about her.

It was the champagne, he told himself as he watched Hayley engage in conversation with the man who fetched them their coats.

She was a beautiful woman and good company. It was natural to enjoy being with her. What man wouldn't?

CHAPTER EIGHT

I'M IN love, I'm in love, I'm in love.

Hayley bounced into the antenatal clinic and Maggie looked up from the desk and raised her eyebrows.

'How much?'

'Sorry?'

'How much have you won? I'm assuming from the look on your face you've won the lottery.' Maggie studied her face and started to laugh. 'Only in this case I suspect the jackpot is a six-foot-two, super-sexy obstetrician called Patrick. Am I right?'

'Don't be ridiculous.' But it was impossible to keep her happiness inside her and Hayley virtually danced round the desk to give Maggie a hug. 'Oh, Maggie, I've never felt like this in my life before. I want to smile and smile. And I... actually I can't put it into words.'

Maggie laughed and hugged her back. 'That's probably a good thing because clinic is about to start.'

'That's why I'm here. The labour ward is really quiet and Jenny said you needed some help down here.' Hayley pulled away from her and realised that her hair hadn't survived the hug. With a grin, she pulled the clasp from her hair, scooped it up and fastened it in her usual haphazard fashion. 'I'll be your wing man. Have I wished you Happy New Year yet? Happy New Year! Where do you want me to start?'

Maggie picked up a set of notes from the pile. 'You can see Olivia. It should be routine but you know the drill anyway. Any problems, yell. Patrick's registrar is doing the clinic because the boss is in some meeting or other. But I expect you know that.'

'Actually, I do, because this morning he was wearing one of his gorgeous suits.' Remembering how good he'd looked as he'd left the house, Hayley smiled dreamily and then pulled herself together. 'Sorry. Where is Olivia?'

'Room 3. Good luck.' Maggie gave a wry smile. 'Olivia talks almost as much as you do.'

After five minutes with the young woman, Hayley was forced to agree.

Olivia had regaled her with everything from her disastrous Christmas to the agonies of morning sickness.

'Honestly, you have no idea.' The woman rolled her eyes. 'I didn't know I'd feel this bad. Other women seem to sail through pregnancy, but I feel as though I've picked up some vile bug that doesn't want to shift.'

'It's like that sometimes,' Hayley murmured sympathetically, checking the height of Olivia's uterus and recording it in the notes. She kept thinking about her evening with Patrick. *The way he'd looked at her across the table.* 'Hopefully it will pass soon and you'll start to feel better.'

'I hope so. I think maybe it's my punishment for all the drinks I had before I knew I was pregnant. This whole thing has come as a shock,' Olivia confessed. 'I'm embarrassed to admit this—*I mean, how stupid can a girl be?*—but I didn't even suspect I could be pregnant. It's not as if we were trying or anything. And I'm not the sort that marks my period on a calendar every month, you know? I'm just not obsessed with that sort of thing.'

'I'm the same,' Hayley said absently, recording the blood-pressure reading and comparing it with the time before, her head somewhere else entirely.

He'd said she was special.

'It just sort of hit me one night. I thought to myself, My period is late. And then I worked out when my last one was and I thought, Oh…' The girl used a word that made Hayley start.

'I can imagine it must have been a bit of a shock.'

'You have no idea.' Olivia rolled her eyes heavenwards. 'I keep telling Mick—he's my boyfriend—well, at least I noticed I was pregnant before I actually delivered. You do hear of women who actually deliver the baby before they find out. I wasn't quite as clueless as that.'

'It isn't always straightforward,' Hayley said tactfully. 'Some women do still have a light period for the first few months and that can delay them realising that they're pregnant.'

'Oh, that didn't happen to me.' Olivia slipped her feet back into her shoes and stood up. 'I had no period at all, but I was basically just too busy to notice. If you're not expecting to be pregnant, you're not looking, are you? I bet you're not like that. You midwives must be really up on stuff like that. I bet no midwife has ever had an unplanned baby. I bet you tick off that date in your calendar every month, just to be sure.'

'I don't go that far.' Hayley laughed. 'But I always know when—' When she was due. And…

Oh, God, she'd missed a period.

The realisation hit her along with a wave of almost crippling nausea and panic.

She'd missed a period. She'd missed a period.

'What's the matter?' Olivia stared at her in alarm. 'Is something wrong? You said everything seemed fine. Are you worried about the baby's growth?'

'No. Nothing. I just…' Frantically she searched for some explanation that would satisfy the patient. 'I just remembered that I had to ring the lab about some results. Not yours. Someone else's.'

How could she not have realised?

She'd been so affronted when Patrick had assumed she was pregnant, it hadn't even occurred to her that she *might* be pregnant. She desperately wanted to go through her diary and check the dates, but Olivia was still chatting.

Somehow Hayley managed to finish the conversation and then she hurried to the desk. 'Maggie, I'm sorry but I have to go to the staff-room for a minute.' Panic engulfed her like rolling clouds and she barely registered Maggie's concerned look before she fled from the department, her heart beating and tears stinging the back of her eyes.

Please, no. Please let her be wrong. Let her have miscalculated, missed a week. Please, please…

The staffroom on the labour ward was empty and she rummaged through her bag and found her diary. Her fingers were shaking so badly it took ages to find November and check the date she needed to know. And as soon as she saw it, she dropped the book back into her bag and stared blankly at the chipped paint on the wall. She didn't need to count twenty-eight days to know that her period was now over a week late. She'd lost track.

She didn't even need to do a pregnancy test.

She knew.

And she also knew that her relationship with Patrick was over.

Pregnancy was no basis for a relationship, was it?

He'd made that clear to her.

And she was very definitely pregnant.

'What do you mean, she just ran out of clinic?' Patrick frowned. 'Was she feeling ill or something?'

'I don't know. Maybe.' Maggie shrugged helplessly. 'Actually, I think she looked more upset than sick, but she didn't say anything to me.'

'Well, that's unusual,' Patrick drawled, 'because Hayley always tells everyone what's on her mind.'

'That's what I love about her,' Maggie said stoutly, and Patrick gave a faint smile.

'And that's why you can stop worrying. As soon as I track her down, she'll tell me what's wrong and we can fix it. At least with Hayley you know where you are.'

'Yes.' Maggie looked at him doubtfully. 'Yes, you're right. Go and find her, Patrick.'

Patrick glanced at the clock. 'I'm due in Theatre in thirty minutes. I have a gynae list.'

'Thirty minutes is ages…' Maggie pushed him towards the door '…and Hayley talks quickly. Go, Patrick. She really did look upset and I'm worried about her.'

Patrick took the stairs to the labour ward, mentally listing the things that could be wrong with Hayley.

They'd had a wonderful evening the night before, but it had been a late night. Was she tired?

Had a patient been rude to her?

Had a member of staff offended her?

Or maybe she was feeling poorly. There were certainly plenty of people off sick with flu.

Pushing open the door of the staffroom, he saw Sally sitting there, talking to Tom.

'Hi, Patrick.' Sally gave a sheepish smile. 'I was bored with the ward so I came up here for a change. How are you doing?'

'Fine, thanks.' Patrick barely registered her. 'Have either of you seen Hayley?'

'No. Why?' Tom frowned. 'Aren't you supposed to be operating?'

'I'm on my way there now.' Patrick paused, frustrated that he hadn't been able to find her. 'If you see Hayley, will you tell her I was looking for her?'

Sally winked at him. 'We certainly will.'

Hayley sat in the toilet, staring down at the test in her hand. It had taken her less than fifteen minutes to grab her coat, sprint to the nearest chemist and buy the test.

And now she was staring at the irrefutable proof that she was pregnant.

She was having Patrick's baby.

How ironic, she thought numbly, that having his baby would mean the end of their relationship. And she knew that it would. Their relationship was too new, too fragile. And given Patrick's past…

It was the cruellest irony.

She couldn't tell him.

She had to keep it from him or he'd feel obliged to do the same thing he'd done with Carly. He was a responsible guy, wasn't he? He'd want to do 'the right thing'.

Only what *was* the right thing?

Marriage certainly hadn't been right for him.

And it hadn't been right for her mother either.

And what about the children? Alfie, Posy and— Hayley rested a hand low on her abdomen—*her baby.*

She knew better than anyone that step-families could be a disaster. She thought of the resentment that her step-siblings had felt when she'd arrived in their family. Did she want to do that to three more children? Alfie and Posy liked her, she knew that. But this was something different entirely. This was *huge*.

She had to make a decision. And she *hated* decisions. And of all the decisions she'd ever had to make in her life, this was the hardest.

Should she tell him? Yes, of course she should. He had a right to know. But if she told him, he'd talk her out of going and it would be for all the wrong reasons.

He didn't want her to be pregnant, she knew that.

Remembering his face when he'd opened the door to her on Christmas Eve, Hayley gave a choked sob. He'd braced himself for hearing that she was pregnant and it was impossible to forget his relief when she'd told him she wasn't. So, knowing that, what choice did she have?

Obviously he adored his children, but he'd made it clear that he didn't want another relationship that was held together only by a pregnancy.

So the right thing to do—the only decision— was to leave.

Pretend their relationship just wasn't working.

And she had no idea how she was supposed to do that convincingly.

How was she supposed to pretend to be miserable?

As the tears dripped onto her hand she almost laughed at herself. She *was* miserable. Horribly miserable. She wouldn't have to act at all. She just needed to not tell him the real reason. For once in her life she had to keep her thoughts locked inside her.

Hayley spread icing on the top of the cup cakes and watched with a lump in her throat as Posy carefully pressed a chocolate button into the centre of each one.

'That's great, Posy,' she said huskily, leaning forwards and hugging the little girl tightly. Her blonde curls smelled of shampoo and the thought of leaving her hurt Hayley almost as much as the thought of leaving Patrick.

'Yum.' Alfie reached out a hand and stole a cake. 'Just one more.' He took a large bite out of the cake and stole a look at Hayley. 'Aren't you going to tell me off? Normally you only let me eat one before tea. You're not acting like yourself.'

She wasn't acting like herself? Obviously she needed to concentrate harder on what she'd usually do. If she wasn't even able to fool the children, how was she going to manage with Patrick?

Before she had time to consider that challenge, she heard his key in the door and dipped her head, pretending to help Posy with the cakes, panic racing through her. He was home really early, which was just going to make the evening longer.

She hoped that for once in her life everything she was feeling wasn't written all over her face.

'Hayley, I've been trying to catch up with you all day.' Patrick slung his coat over the back of the chair and strode across to her. 'Where were you?'

'All over the place. In clinic, then on the labour ward.' Implying that her day had been one mad rush, Hayley smiled at him briefly and then turned her attention back to the chocolate buttons. Never had she paid so much attention to decorating a cake. 'You must have just missed me. How was your theatre list? Any dramas?' *Did she sound normal?* Was she doing OK?

'No dramas.' Patrick kissed Posy on the head, his eyes still on Hayley. 'Are you feeling all right? Maggie said you weren't too good earlier.'

'She's definitely *not* herself,' Alfie said firmly.

'because I've eaten five cakes and she hasn't even noticed.'

Hayley bit back a gasp of horror. Five? He'd eaten *five?* 'I assumed you must be hungry,' she said calmly, desperately hoping he wasn't going to be sick. 'And dinner won't be ready for another twenty minutes. Anyway, you're old enough to judge whether or not you're going to spoil your appetite.'

'I'm only a day older than yesterday,' Alfie said with faultless logic, 'and you didn't think I was old enough to judge then.'

'Well, I'm not going to be around for much longer,' Hayley said brightly, 'so it's good for you to learn not to eat too many cakes in one go.'

Her words were greeted by a stunned silence.

'Wh-what do you mean?' Alfie gaped at her in horror. 'What do you mean you're not going to be around for much longer? Why not? Where are you going?'

'You advertised for a housekeeper for two weeks over Christmas and New Year.' Hayley started to put the cakes carefully into the tin. 'The two weeks is up in a few days' time.'

'But that was before we knew you. Now you're

here, we don't want you to leave after two weeks. We want you to stay for ever!' Alfie was frantic. 'Tell her, Dad! Tell her we want her to stay for ever.'

Hayley knew she ought to speak but the lump in her throat was so huge she knew she was going to embarrass herself.

'We'd like her to stay,' Patrick said carefully. 'Of course we would. She knows that.' His eyes were on her face and Hayley dug her nails into the palms of her hands, wishing she'd come up with a more solid plan for dealing with their protests. But she honestly hadn't known the children would care so much. And as for Patrick…

He wouldn't want her to stay if he knew the truth.

'It's been fantastic.' Somehow she managed to form the words. 'Really—the best Christmas ever. But it was only ever temporary. And so is the work on the unit. I need to get myself a proper job. And I need to visit my family.'

'But your family are mean to you. That's why you didn't want to go there for Christmas.' Alfie was appalled. 'Why would you want to visit them?'

'Well…' Oh, why on earth hadn't she thought

this through? 'Nobody's family is perfect. Now Christmas is over, I ought to see them.'

'You can go and see them and then come straight back.' Alfie looked at his father. 'Dad?'

Patrick stirred. 'Hayley is free to do whatever she wants to do,' he said gruffly, and Alfie gave a choked sob, flung his cake onto the floor and stormed out of the room.

As always, Posy followed, dragging her velvet comforter behind her. 'Alfie sad.'

Hayley stood up immediately, intending to follow, but Patrick took her arm.

'Wait. What's this all about? Why would you want to leave?'

She gave a tiny shrug. 'It was only ever for two weeks and, let's face it, you didn't even want that! It was Alfie's advert.'

'Alfie's advert ceased to be an issue a long time ago. Hayley.' He frowned down at her. 'Tell me what's wrong. Has someone upset you?'

'Gosh, no!' She winced as she heard her falsely bright tone. She wasn't even fooling herself, so how did she hope to fool him? 'Why would you think that? Who could possibly have upset me? Everyone is great. No, I just think it's time to move on. It's been fantastic, Patrick. A fantastic Christmas. This barn is just the perfect place, it's just been—'

'Fantastic. Yes, I got that. You've said it three times already. What I really want to hear is all the things you're *not* saying.' Patrick's mouth tightened and his eyes were suddenly searching. 'Is this about us?'

'Us?' How was she supposed to respond to that? OK, so definitely *not* like Hayley. She tried to work out what a twenty-first-century woman would say. What would Diane, her stepsister, say? 'It was fun while it lasted, Patrick. But we both knew it wasn't practical in the long term. We both have our own lives to lead. You have the children.'

'I thought you liked the children.' Patrick's tone was cautious. 'I was under the impression you liked them quite a lot.'

'They're gorgeous!' *Rubbish answer,* Hayley, she thought to herself. *You're thinking like yourself, not like Diane.* With a huge effort she forced herself to say words that were so alien it was almost impossible to voice them. 'But I don't know how you do it, Patrick. I mean, you have no time to yourself. No time to chill out. They're always *there!*'

And she loved that. *She really loved that.*

'Yes.' His voice was strangely flat and he released her suddenly. 'They are always there.'

'And I suppose I'm just used to being single. Needing my space.' Oh, God, she was useless at this. Utterly useless. And she needed to get out of here before she blew it totally. 'Well, anyway, talking of space—I must go and take a bath. A long soaky bath. It's been a long day.'

His gaze didn't shift from her face and Hayley was suddenly terrified that she had *Pregnant* written on her forehead.

He was an obstetrician, for goodness' sake, and a skilled one at that. What if he could diagnose pregnancy from a distance?

Why didn't he say something?

She carried on babbling. 'I might not join you this evening if you don't mind.' For a start, she wasn't sure she could make it through the evening without sobbing, and on top of that she needed to start acting like a woman who found children a bit much. 'I'm in the middle of a really good book. I might just sprawl on the bed—you know, veg out, generally relax and do nothing.'

Still he didn't respond and still his gaze didn't

shift from her face. It was as if he was looking for something.

'The casserole should be ready by now and I did baked potatoes.' Her voice tailed off under the intensity of his blue gaze. 'So, I'll say good-night, then, just in case I don't see you later.'

She slunk towards the door, heard Alfie crying and fought a desperate urge to go to him. How could she go to him when she'd just claimed that she wanted a child-free evening? But the fact that she couldn't comfort the little boy—the fact that she was the cause of his tears—made everything even worse.

She was doing it for them, Hayley reminded herself miserably when she eventually slid into the bath and let the tears fall freely.

She was doing it for them.

In the long run, it would be better.

CHAPTER NINE

'SHE'S leaving? Why would she leave? *What did you do to her?*' Maggie stood in front of Patrick's desk like a sergeant major in a court-martial.

'Maggie.' He dragged his gaze from the computer screen. 'I don't have time for this now.'

'Then make time, Patrick Buchannan, because if you let that girl leave this unit, I swear I'll resign too!'

Patrick sighed. 'I know she's a good midwife, but I can't force her to take a job here.'

'But she's leaving because of you! And I want to know why!'

'I don't know why!' Exploding with tension and frustration, Patrick rose to his feet and paced to the far end of his office. 'Damn it, Maggie, *I don't know why!*'

Maggie looked startled. 'You don't? I assumed—'

'You assumed what? That we'd had a row?' Patrick gave a bitter laugh and turned to stare out of the window. The day was bleak and cold and totally in keeping with his current mood. 'I wish we had had a row. At least then I would have known what it was about. But this is—'

'Something happened yesterday in the clinic.' Maggie sat down in Patrick's chair, a frown on her face. 'She came bouncing in, told me that she was in love with you and then she—'

'Wait a minute.' Patrick turned, his gaze sharp. 'She told you she was in love with me?'

'Yes. Well, virtually. Yes, definitely. Patrick, she's *crazy* about you. Surely you don't need me to tell you that.'

Patrick considered the evidence. 'Up until last night I would have agreed with you, but…' he shook his head '…she virtually said she'd had enough of living her life around the children. That it was a massive sacrifice.'

'Hayley adores children,' Maggie scoffed, 'and she especially adores yours. She talks about nothing else. All day we have to listen to tales of

what Posy has drawn and the funny things Alfie
has said. She's worse than you are.'

'Thanks,' Patrick said dryly, and Maggie grinned.

'No offence meant. But what I'm saying is that
Hayley is as crazy about your children as she is
about you.'

'Maybe, but that doesn't mean that living with
them constantly isn't a strain. They're full on,
Maggie. They're all over her. In her bed, wrapped
around her in the evenings—she can't even go to
the bathroom without Posy banging on the door.'
Patrick sighed. 'Last night Alfie was crying and
she didn't go to him.'

Maggie looked startled. 'She let him cry?'

'Well…' Patrick ran his hand over the back
of his neck '…she left the room. Said she
needed a bath or something. Wanted to read her
book.'

'In other words, she couldn't bear to hear him
crying and not comfort him.' Maggie folded her
arms. 'If you ask me, Hayley thinks she has to
leave and she's doing everything she can to make
it seem as though she wants to.'

'What?' Patrick was totally confused. 'Is that
female logic? Because if so, could it please come

with a translation? I have no idea what you're talking about.'

'For an incredibly intelligent man, you can be very dim.' Maggie stood up and walked across the room until she was standing in front of him. 'Hayley is in love with you. That is a fact. I know you haven't known each other very long, I know it's all been a bit whirlwind, but she is definitely in love with you. She is also in love with your children. If she's talking about leaving then it's because something has happened.' She frowned. 'Or maybe because something hasn't happened. Did you propose to her?'

'Of course I didn't propose to her!' Patrick looked at his colleague in incredulous disbelief. 'Maggie, I can't believe we're having this conversation.'

'Well, you obviously weren't getting anywhere by yourself. Could that be the problem? Have you told her that you love her?'

'I— No, I haven't because I don't even know that I...' Patrick rubbed his fingers across his forehead. 'Maggie, I've been married before—'

'To a woman you didn't love. And that was *entirely* different.'

'I've only known Hayley for a few weeks.'

'And in that time you have more feeling for her than you ever did for your wife.'

Stunned, Patrick let his hand drop. 'How do you know that?'

'Because Christmas is a bad time of year for you, my friend,' Maggie said softly. 'And suddenly, this year, it's all different. You're smiling. You're relaxed. Your children are smiling and relaxed. Ask yourself why, Patrick. And then do something about it. Quickly. Before it's too late.'

'I'll go and prepare the pool for you, Ruth,' Hayley said. 'You might like to take a walk up the corridor and back again. It's good to keep moving at this stage of your labour. I'll only be in the room across the way, but if you need anything, just press the buzzer.'

Feeling exhausted and slightly sick, she took refuge in the empty room opposite.

As she prepared the pool, she pondered on the fact that this was her last shift.

She really ought to ring her mother and warn her that she was coming home tomorrow, but she couldn't face the conversation.

Neither could she face the thought of moving out of Patrick's house.

Of leaving the children.

Tears filled her eyes and she tested the temperature of the water, barely able to see the thermometer. Oh, this was ridiculous! If this was what being pregnant was like, she'd better buy shares in a tissue company.

'Hayley?' Patrick's voice came from the doorway and she realised with a start of horror that she'd been so preoccupied in her own misery that she hadn't even heard the door open.

How long had he been standing there?

Did he know she was crying?

'Just doing the pool, Patrick,' she said brightly. 'Did you want me?'

Oh, for goodness' sake, she'd done it again! Used the wrong words at absolutely the wrong time.

'Yes, I want you.' His tone was firm. Steady. 'I thought we'd already established that. I also thought we'd established that you want me, too.'

Hayley blinked back tears and concentrated on the surface of the pool. 'Patrick, this really isn't a good time. We should—'

'I have something to say to you and I want you to listen.'

Hayley froze. He was probably going to tell her that she'd upset Alfie. 'Honestly, I really don't— Can we talk later?'

'No.' He was right behind her and he drew her to her feet, turning her so that she faced him. 'There are things I want to say to you, and they can't wait. I love you, Hayley.' His voice soft, Patrick took her face in his hands and forced her to look at him. 'I love you, sweetheart.'

No, not that.

He couldn't be saying that to her. Not here. *Not now.*

Before she'd discovered she was pregnant, *I love you* were the words she'd been desperate to hear, but now they were the words she was desperate *not* to hear because hearing them just made everything so much worse.

'Patrick—'

'I haven't finished. There's something else I want to say to you.' He let his hands drop and when he lifted them again he was holding a velvet box. 'I want you to marry me. I want you to be my wife.'

Her hands still wet from the pool water,

Hayley stared at the box in stunned silence and then at his face.

She stared into those blue eyes and then back down at the box. 'You— I...'

With a soft laugh he opened the box and removed a ring. A beautiful diamond solitaire. 'Marry me, Hayley.' He took the ring out of the box, slid it onto her finger—and she didn't even stop him.

For a moment—just for a moment—she wanted to know what that ring would look like on her finger. *She wanted to dream.*

And then she remembered that dreams only happened while you were asleep. That was why they were called dreams.

And she was wide awake.

'I can't marry you, Patrick,' she said in a choked voice. 'I can't do that.' She sensed his shock.

'I know it's a bit sudden,' he said carefully. 'I know we haven't known each other that long—but it's right, Hayley. You know it is. Say yes.'

'I can't, Patrick.' She stared down at the ring he'd placed on her finger. It sparkled under the lights, the diamond winking at her, as if taunting her with what she couldn't have. 'I can't marry you, Patrick.'

'Is this because of what I said to you the day you arrived? I know I was tactless and insensitive.' He gave a rueful smile. 'I know I upset you by assuming you must be pregnant—'

'Patrick, I *am* pregnant.' Her voice rose. '*I am pregnant*, OK? I'm pregnant, pregnant, pregnant. I'm having your baby. So *now* do you understand that it's all hopeless? All of it. And it can't ever work.' Tears falling down her cheeks, she tugged at the ring—*the ring that had been on her finger for less than two minutes*—and pushed it blindly into his hand.

She waited for him to say something but he was silent and his silence was like a vicious blow.

What had she expected?

She'd *known* what his reaction would be.

'Please.' She gave up waiting for him to speak. 'Please—do me a favour and don't come back on the labour ward while I'm here. I just can't— I need to pull myself together— I won't be unprofessional.' She wiped her eyes on the back of her hand and made for the door. 'As soon as this shift is over, I'll go home and pack. I'm sorry, Patrick. I'm sorry for all of it.'

* * *

Ruth didn't deliver until the early hours of the morning and Hayley stayed with her, offering support, enjoying her moment of happiness, which was even more poignant given how thrilled Ruth's husband was.

Afterwards she drank a cup of tea on her own in the staffroom, wondering what would happen when her time came.

Would she be alone? Or would some kind midwife be willing to sit with her through the night while she laboured?

It was still dark outside when she finally arrived back at Patrick's barn and Hayley crept up to her bedroom, packed her one small suitcase and lay fully clothed on top of the bed until it seemed like a reasonable time to call a taxi.

Maybe she was being cowardly, leaving while everyone was still in bed, but she couldn't face an emotional departure.

She'd written letters to the children and left them on the table in the kitchen. She'd tried to write a letter to Patrick but after about fifty attempts she'd given up.

At some point they'd have to talk, of course. They needed to sort out what they were going to do. He'd want access to his child and she wanted that, too. She didn't want their child growing up not knowing his or her father.

And she'd do the right thing. Make it as easy as she could for everyone—try and get a job close by. Not too local—that would be asking too much—but close enough.

The crunch of tyres in the drive told her that the taxi had arrived and she took a last look around the barn before stepping out into the snow and closing the door behind her.

Jack, the taxi driver, waved from the car and she waved back, hoping he wasn't going to ask her too many questions. Hayley felt as though she'd lived a whole life since he'd first dropped her here two weeks earlier.

She was four steps down the path when her legs went in different directions.

'Oh, for—' Bracing herself for impact, she screwed up her face but this time powerful arms caught her, lifting her upright before she hit the ground.

'I don't know how you think you're going to manage without me,' Patrick drawled. 'You can't even walk if I'm not there to catch you.'

Her heart pounding, Hayley clutched at him as he steadied her. 'I didn't know you were awake.'

'I haven't been to sleep. Have you?'

'Well, no.' She doubted she'd ever sleep again. The misery inside her felt so great she had no idea how she was going to cope. 'Patrick, I have to go. Jack is waiting.'

'He's all right for a minute—you're not running away from me, Hayley. Not before we've talked.' Patrick was still holding her, his hands firm on her arms. 'And we have lots to talk about.'

'I know. I *know* we're going to have to talk at some point, but I can't do it now. I need some time—'

'Time for what?'

'Time to think! Time to—I don't know. Time to get over you.'

Patrick inhaled sharply. 'Why would you want to get over me?'

'Because we can't be together.' Her voice was clogged. 'And having your baby is difficult, but it's my problem and I'll sort it out.'

'Problem?' He frowned, his eyes searching hers. 'You haven't told me how you feel about being pregnant. Is it a problem, sweetheart? Is that how you feel?'

Her heart turned over. 'No, of course not. It's just…' *Just because of us,* was what she wanted to say. But what was the point?

'Hayley, I don't want you to "get over" me.' His lean handsome face was unusually pale, his voice ragged. 'I want you to marry me. I told you that yesterday.'

'I *can't* marry you, you know that.'

'I don't know that.' His eyes shimmered with raw intensity. 'I love you and at first I couldn't work out why you would possibly say no when I know you love me, too. I spent the night thinking about it. I spent the night thinking, *Why would she turn me down?*'

'Patrick, you *know* why.'

'When did you discover you were pregnant, Hayley?'

'Yesterday morning in clinic.'

His eyebrows rose. 'And you didn't say anything to anyone? The one time you need some support— the time you needed to talk—you kept it a secret?'

'It was too big to share.'

Patrick muttered something under his breath. '*Nothing* is ever too big for us to share.'

'This was. I didn't know how to tell you,' Hayley said huskily, 'What was the *point* in telling you?'

'I can't believe you just said that.' Patrick's grip didn't ease. 'It took me most of the night to work out why you would turn me down, Hayley. And then I realised that it's my fault. The reason you won't marry me is because of what happened with Carly, isn't it?'

'Yes. Partly.' She didn't deny it. 'A baby isn't a reason to get married, Patrick. You told me that.'

'And I stand by that. It's true. A baby isn't a reason to get married. But the baby isn't the reason I asked you to marry me.'

'Of course it is. You said that—'

'I proposed to you before I knew you were pregnant, Hayley.'

She opened her mouth and closed it again. Then opened it. But nothing came out.

Patrick gave a faint smile. 'You're doing it again. Staying silent when I need to know what you're thinking. I never thought I'd have to say this to you, but could you please start talking?'

'Patrick…' Words failed her and he sighed.

'That night in Chicago was incredible. I couldn't stop thinking about it. I couldn't stop thinking about *you*. I even contemplated getting in touch with you but I had no idea what I'd say. I'd decided that it wasn't fair to drag the children to the States, and I couldn't ask you to come here. And when I opened my door on Christmas Eve and you were standing there…'

'You thought I was pregnant,' Hayley whispered. 'And you were shocked.'

'Yes,' he said honestly. 'I'd made that mistake before and I wasn't going to make it again. But then I got to know you.'

'It's only been a couple of weeks—'

'Yes. And those weeks have been incredible. You transformed our lives with your sunny personality, your goodness and your non-stop chatter. You made us happy. And I thought you were happy, too.'

Her eyes stinging, Hayley smiled. 'I was happy. Very happy.'

'Then why are you leaving?'

'Because I'm pregnant and that changes everything.'

'I asked you to marry me because I love you. *Not* because you're having my baby. And I'm asking you again now, for the same reason.' His hands shifted from her arms to her face and he gazed down at her. 'I love you. I want to be with you. Will you marry me?'

'Say yes, love,' Jack yelled from the taxi, and Hayley gave a gasp of horror and buried her face in Patrick's coat.

'He can hear us?'

'Every word,' Patrick said calmly, 'and I really couldn't care less. It's your answer I want, not his.'

'Patrick—'

'Answer me one question.' He lifted her chin with his fingers and for once his voice wasn't completely steady. 'Do you love me?'

She gazed into his blue eyes, suddenly shy. 'Yes, of course I do. You know that.'

'How much?'

'As much as it's possible to love someone. I'm crazy about you. Do you really have to ask? I gave up everything to come here, Patrick. I gave up my job, my flat—I made a complete fool of myself over you. I followed my dream.'

With a groan he lowered his head to hers, his

kiss unusually tender. 'Now answer me another question.' He murmured the words against her mouth, his eyes holding hers. 'Do you love my children?'

'I *adore* your children!'

'Then what's the problem?'

Distracted by the kiss, it took Hayley a moment to answer. 'Pregnancy isn't a good reason to get married.'

'We've just established that I proposed *before* I knew you were pregnant.'

Unable to argue with that, she pulled away slightly. 'It isn't just you, Patrick,' she confessed softly. 'It's me, too. I mean, I was brought up in a stepfamily and frankly it was *awful*. Dysfunctional just doesn't begin to describe it. All right, we love each other—but that might not be enough! It isn't just about us, is it? It's about Alfie and Posy and how they might feel about the baby. What if they resent it?'

'We won't resent it!' Alfie was standing in the doorway, shivering in his dressing gown, Posy in his arms. 'We can't wait for you to marry Daddy and give us a baby brother or sister, can we, Pose? Well, Posy doesn't really know, of course, because she's still little and only interested in her blanket, but also because she hasn't had a sister yet, and I have. It's great.' He frowned. 'Well, maybe not the nappy part, that's pretty gross actually, but the rest of it is cool.'

Hayley gave a cry of concern. 'How long have you been standing there? Alfie, you must be *freezing*.'

'We've been here long enough to hear everything. We're a family, Hayley. Team Buchannan. You should join our team.' Alfie shifted Posy awkwardly. 'Dad is a pretty good catch. All the women around here want him.'

Hayley bit back a laugh. 'You've only known me for a couple of weeks. Why would you want me to be on your team?'

'Well, there's the obvious stuff of course— you can cook well, and you're great at clearing up after us. And then there's the fact that two of the kittens are yours so if you stay we get to keep all four, which would be cool. But the real reason is because we love you and we know you love Dad.' Alfie hitched Posy up in his arms. 'I heard you say you love him. Mum never said that. Not once. I heard her say loads of stuff to

Dad, but she never said *I love you*. You *do* love Dad, I can tell. And he loves you. And so do we. And do you mind if I go in now, because Posy weighs a ton? It must be all the turkey she's eaten.' Staggering slightly, he backed into the house, leaving Hayley with tears pouring down her cheeks.

'I can't believe he just said all that.' She was humbled by the children's warmth and acceptance.

'Do you really think our family isn't going to work?' Laughing, Patrick took her hand and slid the ring back onto her finger. 'We're not going to let you say no, Hayley. We want you on Team Buchannan. Say yes. Come on—of all the words I've heard you say, that's the one I want to hear.'

Hayley looked around her. She looked at the beautiful barn, the mountains and the snow-covered trees. And then she looked at the man standing in front of her—*the man she loved.*

'You do realise that Alfie is right—if you marry me you'll end up keeping all four kittens,' she said, and her voice wobbled. 'He gave them to me as a present and I won't be parted from them.'

Patrick rolled his eyes, but he was smiling. 'I think I can probably cope.'

'You're sure you don't want more time to think about it?'

'I'm sure. I love you, Hayley, that isn't going to change.'

'In that case, yes,' she said in a choked voice. 'Yes, of course. I'll marry you. Oh, Patrick…' She flung her arms round his neck and Jack beeped the horn madly and cheered.

'Good job I don't have any neighbours,' Patrick drawled, his mouth against hers as he kissed her again. 'Given that he knows such a lot about your underwear, I think perhaps we'd better invite Jack to the wedding. What do you think?'

'I think I love you, Patrick Buchannan,' Hayley said huskily. 'I think I love you with all my heart.'

MEDICAL™

Large Print

Titles for the next six months...

July

POSH DOC, SOCIETY WEDDING	Joanna Neil
THE DOCTOR'S REBEL KNIGHT	Melanie Milburne
A MOTHER FOR THE ITALIAN'S TWINS	Margaret McDonagh
THEIR BABY SURPRISE	Jennifer Taylor
NEW BOSS, NEW-YEAR BRIDE	Lucy Clark
GREEK DOCTOR CLAIMS HIS BRIDE	Margaret Barker

August

EMERGENCY: PARENTS NEEDED	Jessica Matthews
A BABY TO CARE FOR	Lucy Clark
PLAYBOY SURGEON, TOP-NOTCH DAD	Janice Lynn
ONE SUMMER IN SANTA FE	Molly Evans
ONE TINY MIRACLE...	Carol Marinelli
MIDWIFE IN A MILLION	Fiona McArthur

September

THE DOCTOR'S LOST-AND-FOUND BRIDE	Kate Hardy
MIRACLE: MARRIAGE REUNITED	Anne Fraser
A MOTHER FOR MATILDA	Amy Andrews
THE BOSS AND NURSE ALBRIGHT	Lynne Marshall
NEW SURGEON AT ASHVALE A&E	Joanna Neil
DESERT KING, DOCTOR DADDY	Meredith Webber

MILLS & BOON®

MEDICAL™

Large Print

October

THE NURSE'S BROODING BOSS	Laura Iding
EMERGENCY DOCTOR AND CINDERELLA	Melanie Milburne
CITY SURGEON, SMALL TOWN MIRACLE	Marion Lennox
BACHELOR DAD, GIRL NEXT DOOR	Sharon Archer
A BABY FOR THE FLYING DOCTOR	Lucy Clark
NURSE, NANNY…BRIDE!	Alison Roberts

November

THE SURGEON'S MIRACLE	Caroline Anderson
DR DI ANGELO'S BABY BOMBSHELL	Janice Lynn
NEWBORN NEEDS A DAD	Dianne Drake
HIS MOTHERLESS LITTLE TWINS	Dianne Drake
WEDDING BELLS FOR THE VILLAGE NURSE	Abigail Gordon
HER LONG-LOST HUSBAND	Josie Metcalfe

December

THE MIDWIFE AND THE MILLIONAIRE	Fiona McArthur
FROM SINGLE MUM TO LADY	Judy Campbell
KNIGHT ON THE CHILDREN'S WARD	Carol Marinelli
CHILDREN'S DOCTOR, SHY NURSE	Molly Evans
HAWAIIAN SUNSET, DREAM PROPOSAL	Joanna Neil
RESCUED: MOTHER AND BABY	Anne Fraser

MILLS & BOON®